Into the Rabbit Hole

The Sacred Stones

In scientia fidei robur

Nisi qui habet scientiam in fide

Book 2

Books by Micah T. Dank

Into the Rabbit Hole *series*

Book 1: Beneath the Veil

Book 2: The Sacred Stones

Coming Soon!

Book 3: The Secret Weapon

Book 4: Pangaeas Pandemic

Book 5: The Hidden Archives

Book 6: The Final Type

Into the Rabbit Hole

The Sacred Stones

Book 2

Micah T. Dank

SPEAKING VOLUMES, LLC
NAPLES, FLORIDA
2020

The Sacred Stones

ISBN 978-1-64540-284-8

This book is dedicated to two dear friends William Devine and John Ardolino, who have both in their own way, convinced me to expand my one book into six, and encouraged me to dig deeper than I ever have before.

To Tucker Max and the cast of the Jersey Shore for showing me how to go wild in my 20's and how to settle down in my 30's. Thank you all.

Finally, to my second mom Margaret O'Keefe,
I will always love and miss you.

Astrology is a language. If you understand this language, the sky speaks to you – Dane Rudhyar

Chapter One

I'm swimming through the Grand Canal in Venice, underwater in scuba gear. After getting lost, I have about 20% oxygen left in my tank, but I'm almost at the Ca' Sagredo Hotel. I don't know if I'll have enough oxygen to get back to Rosette and them once I pick up the cargo. If I don't, I'll have to come to the surface, where I'll get arrested for what I will have in my possession, and the Vatican will get involved. Well, more involved than they have been in my life so far. It's amazing I've lasted this long.

Swimming towards the hotel, I start thinking about the Zodiac and how it pertains to religion. Nerds would have loved to hear me tell them what I recently figured out. If you picture the signs of the Zodiac, you can see how they are different names for God's son, or should I say, "sun." He's called the 'Scape*goat* of Israel,' Capricorn. He's the 'Son of man,' the man sign Aquarius. He's the 'Fisherman of men,' Pisces the two fish. He's the 'Lamb of God,' or the ram in Aries. He's called 'The strong bull,' or the bull in Taurus. Should I keep going?

St. Augustine said of him, 'My own good beetle,' or the 'original beetle' from James' letter: Cancer, the crab. He's the 'Lion of Judah' also known as Leo. The lady holding the stalk of wheat, Virgo. He's born of a virgin and he's called 'the bread of life.' Libra, the scales of justice. He's known as, 'The just one.' I'm not going into the rest of them, but you get the picture. It's also why He's worshipped on Sunday. But I digress. That's old news.

I'm basically snorkeling through a sewage system. It's also freezing cold. The summer is actually when the water is coldest because it spent all fall, winter, and spring cooling off. Ironically, the winter is when the water is warmest.

The key is to make sure nobody sees me moving through this canal of piss and crap. My heart is racing, which in turn is making me breathe harder and use more oxygen than I'd like to at this time.

Shit, I'm sorry. . . I just realized you have no idea what's going on right now or how we ended up on this chase. I'll have to backpedal a bit to get you up to speed. I thought the last time was the adventure of a lifetime, but I had no idea that things would get so much deeper this time around.

Chapter Two

Three months earlier

"Who gave you this letter?" I asked my producer.

"You wouldn't believe me even if I told you," he said. He was always playing these kinds of dumb games with me.

"I need to know, so can you just cut the bull?" I snapped.

"This came from the Souza-Baranowski Correctional Center. I wasn't going to ask questions, but do you have any idea who it's from?" he asked.

There was only one person it could have come from, but I couldn't wrap my head around it. Why he would reach out to me? I started to get dizzy and went to the cooler for a cup of water. Then I flipped my phone open and gave Rosette a call, telling her to meet me back at the house.

That's another thing; Hannah and I bought a small ranch house in Quincy, Massachusetts, not far from the Red Line. Rosette and her boyfriend had basically moved in on the weekends.

Yup, I forgot to mention that as well. Rosette had somehow, in between all the tragedy, become rather close with a Physics TA she met at Boston College named Jackson Rider. He sounds like a porn star with that name, but, to be fair, he looks like one too. A tall, muscular mulatto boy, the kind of person who makes you wonder if you are a little gay yourself. Personally, it doesn't matter if you're black or white. See what I just did there? I'm just messing with you. But somehow between her swim meets at BC and being in an accelerated Psychology program, she managed to find this guy and they've been nothing but great together.

It took me forty-five minutes to get back home on Summer Street. Mostly because I was stopped repeatedly along the way by kids who recognized me from the radio and wanted to talk. It's great being a D-list local celebrity, isn't it? I don't think I'll ever get used to the attention I get from it.

I grabbed a slice at the corner pizzeria and went home. I've been weaning myself off of organic food after I heard Blur talking about how there was only a modicum of difference between GMOs and Organic.

"What's up, Newsdon?" Rosette chirped. She's had a permanent grin on her face since she met Jackson.

"Nothing much, Rose. Listen, I gotta talk to you guys about something. I'm not sure how much Jackson knows regarding the last year so . . ." I trailed off as she interrupted me.

"He knows everything. I wasn't going to keep any secrets from him, especially because you told me that it's not over," she said.

"Graham, it's all good, baby. Just lay it on us," Jackson said.

"Thanks Jackson, that means a lot, especially since you know how crazy the last year has been for all of us," Hannah said.

"So, I got a letter in the mail from Souza-Baranowski Correctional Center," I said.

"Who the hell do you know there?" Rosette asked.

"I have no idea. It was addressed to me but no name on it. Well, I think I might know, but it doesn't make sense for a few reasons," I said.

"Well, what did it say?" Jackson asked.

"The key to all wisdom is in the missing capstone to the pyramids," I replied.

"Can I see the letter?" Hannah asked.

"Sure love," and gave it to her.

"What does this mean, it all begins at Christ the Redeemer?" she asked.

"I've been trying to figure that out myself. I have no idea," I replied. I didn't tell them yet that there was another piece of paper in the envelope addressed to me. The problem was, it was blank, and I couldn't figure out what it was for exactly. Was I supposed to reply and send it back with it?

"This letter makes no sense. Was there anything more that came along with it?" Hannah said.

"Actually, there was—this blank sheet of paper came with it," I replied.

"A blank sheet of paper? What's the point of that?" Jackson replied.

"I've been trying to figure that one out since I got this at the radio station," I said.

"Something doesn't feel right about this at all, Newsdon. Nothing that we've dealt with over the past year was done without intent and purpose. Can I see that paper?" Rosette asked.

"Knock yourself out," I replied.

She took the paper from me and looked at both sides of it. "This doesn't make any sense," she said, setting it down on the table.

"If you were going to get a message out from jail where they review everything before it goes, what would be the best way to do it?" Rosette pondered.

"I'd leave a cryptic message," Hannah said.

"Right, so what are we missing here?" Rosette replied.

"I'll be right back, I need to clear my head," I said. I took a walk down the block to pick up a soda at the corner store. *Come on, think Graham, somebody obviously thinks that we have the ability to put two and two together here.* I grabbed a diet Dr. Pepper and went to the register.

"Hey, how are you doing?" I asked the cashier.

"I'm fine thanks, and how are you?" she replied, smiling. "Would you like to buy one of our new scratch and sniff scratch off tickets that just came in?" she asked.

"No thanks, I think I'm fine . . ." I responded, my voice trailing off. Wait, scratch and sniff? Did I miss something? The paper that was sent to us was a little stiff. I suddenly had a crazy idea. I ran back to the house and found everyone in the living room, trying still to figure this all out.

"No soda for any of us? Cold-blooded, Graham," Jackson said.

"Can I see that paper one more time?" I asked.

"Sure," Jackson said, and passed it to me.

I picked the paper up and smelled it. It smelled like lemon. I put my tongue to it, and sure enough, it also tasted like lemon.

"What are you doing, honey?" Hannah asked.

"If you were in jail and were trying to get a message out, what would be the simplest way to do it?" I asked.

"I suppose you'd hide the message," Jackson said.

"Correct, but now watch this," I said.

I took the paper and turned on the light, carefully removing the lampshade. I put the paper up to the light, but not too close. After a few seconds, words began to form on the paper.

What do the Robert E. Lee Memorial, the Jefferson Memorial, Christ Church, Mt. Vernon Square, Washington Circle, Dupont Circle and Logan Circle have in common? You'd be surprised. Follow the dollar.

"Well, what do those have in common?" Rosette asked. "Follow the dollar? Are they talking about how they were funded?"

"I have no idea. Maybe it has something to do with the Christ Church? Christ the Redeemer? Maybe that's what is being referenced here?" I asked.

We discussed this a little longer, but we were running out of ideas. I still couldn't believe I was given a coded letter from jail. I was eventually going to have to address the elephant in the room, which was why I had received a letter from jail to begin with. But right now we had to figure this out.

Robert E. Lee Memorial and Jefferson Memorial. Could it be the wars from their time period and who funded them? Was that what was meant by following the money? I also couldn't shake the feeling that Christ

Church and Christ the Redeemer had parts to play. But what exactly? We just figured out that the Bible was encoded and that both Judeo-Christian religions were piggybacking off of older religions and the stars. What more could either of them possibly have to offer? Follow the dollar, it said. I took a dollar bill from out of my wallet and tried to figure out what the hell he was talking about.

"I think we need to lay the points out on a map, Graham," Jackson said.

"Yeah Rider, that's a pretty solid idea," Rosette said. She always referred to people by their last names—I have no idea why.

"Yeah, you know what, I still have a map of DC from my last trip there with the one we don't speak of," I said. "I'll be right back."

I went into our bedroom and found the map in a drawer. Ran back out to where everyone was still sitting around the dining room table.

"OK, so here is a map of unfiltered DC."

"So, the next step would be to map the points, right?" Hannah asked.

I carefully took a marker and mapped out the points mentioned in the letter.

"It looks like a pyramid," Rosette squealed.

"Not quite, it's missing the top. Wait, is this what he meant by the missing capstones of the pyramid?" I asked.

"But why follow the dollar then?" Jackson asked as he took a dollar bill out of his pocket and put it on the table next to the map.

All at once I saw it. I had only looked at the dollar from the front, completely ignoring the back. It's the pyramid, or should I say the unfinished pyramid on the left side.

"This is the *All Seeing Eye* of the Illuminati," I observed. "The text says, 'New World Order' in Latin."

"Newsdon, the pyramid is detached on the dollar," Rosette chimed in.

"Correct, but look at the map of DC with these focal points." I showed everyone the map and it, too, was an unfinished pyramid. "Follow the dollar the letter said, so let's superimpose the all seeing eye onto the map," I finished.

It took us a while to find a picture of DC, as most maps do not show much above what we already had. But after taking in the dimensions of the dollar and figuring out the dimensions of the map, we were finally able to superimpose the *All Seeing Eye*, or the Eye of Horus in Egyptian times. What was at the center of the eye? The Grand Lodge of the Freemasons on MacArthur Boulevard, also known as the House of the Temple.

If you look at the lodge, it also has an unfinished pyramid on its top. Also thinking back to the dollar bill, the front of it was George Washington, who was one of the first Freemasons in this country.

This had to be it. I realized then that we had a friend who actually was a Mason: a guy named Josh, from my days at Georgetown. He was in the SABs with me and he who is not to be named.

"Feel like taking a trip to DC, Jackson?" I asked.

He instantly agreed, but only if he could drive. He did not want to take a ride on Amtrak. Fortunately, I hate driving.

I recently heard Blur talking about the General Motors streetcar conspiracy where they hatched a plan to buy and destroy streetcar systems in most US cities so that the car industry could take off. Sure, you still have streetcars in Boston and San Francisco, but because of this, everybody ended up needing to have a car to get around. There's also a study that was done decades ago where they were able to correlate the lead in gasoline to rising violent crime and murder rates, and when they banned the lead, it went down. Sounds insane, but it's true.

Jackson had never been to DC before. I was going to have to let my frat brothers know we would need a place to crash for the night. At what age is it appropriate to stop visiting your little's little's little and just move on from frat life? Oh well, that would be another day.

"Be safe, baby," Hannah said.

"Take care of Rider, will you, Newsdon?" Rosette said.

I packed and hopped in the car with Jackson to go back to Chestnut Hill. We left Rosette and Hannah alone. They'd probably have a girly weekend together, loving the short break from us. The one thing I did not count on was how terrified Josh was going to be when we came to him with what we were given, and how far we were going to have to go if we wanted to see this through.

You stop explaining yourself when you realize people only understand from their level of perception. – Jim Carrey

Chapter Three

Would you believe it took us nine hours to get from Boston to DC? We pulled up on Bouillon Square and parked a few houses down. This was ground zero for debauchery and I didn't want any drunks puking or pissing on Jackson's car. I called brother Tommy's cell phone, and, within a minute, we were let in. It was a quiet week for the frat, with nothing crazy going on. We went in and a few games of flip cup and beer pong were in progress. We set up shop in my old room. The new brother living there was out for the weekend. Last time I was here, I first read my brother James' final letter to me and drunkenly washed it away. One drink to remember, and another to forget, right? I called my old friend Josh, and he agreed to meet us. We left the frat house and took a cab to the lodge on MacArthur. Josh opened the door. Before he could say anything, I began talking.

"What exactly are the unfinished pyramids?" I asked him.

His face turned white as a ghost as he closed the door behind him. "Graham, you can't just come in and blurt shit like that out loud, especially not here."

"That doesn't change my question, Josh. This is Jackson by the way. Rosette's boyfriend."

"Pleased to meet you," Jackson said.

"Likewise," Josh shot back. "Graham, you have to understand something. The missing capstones are an urban legend. Many have tried to find them and all of them have come up empty-handed. There's no real proof that they even exist. I can't help you with this," Josh said.

"Why not?" I asked.

"I could lose my membership here and from all other societies I might want to join. This is like the black sheep of society information," he finished, looking worried that I had even brought this up.

"Come on Josh, you have to give me something here. I received a coded letter in the mail after all that stuff happened months ago. I can't just drop this," I said.

"I wish I could help you my friend, but I can't," he exhaled. "But I know someone who might be able to."

"Who?"

"Reach out to Blur Slanders, he'll know about this if anyone does," he said.

"Seriously?" I shot him a look. He hated Blur Slanders like most people in this world, despite the fact that he would tell some pretty great truths. I suddenly got a flashback of my friend NP's endless hours of watching him on TV and got an overwhelming urge to go to the bar. "So that's it?"

"Afraid so. I have to be heading back. I'm sorry you wasted your time, Graham. Nice seeing you, though." Josh walked back into the lodge.

"Well, this was a complete waste of time," Jackson said.

"Couldn't agree more. Come on, let's get back to the girls," I said.

We didn't even spend the night in DC. I wondered as we started the car ride if I could have just called Josh and asked him. Actually, the way the government stores cell phone transcripts, he might have given us even less. I flipped my phone open, Googled Blur Slanders, and got the number to call into his show. I called it and was on hold for 40 minutes. Finally, a screener picked up and asked my name. Luckily, he recognized me from the DC funeral and the uploaded video from Lilac Northinly's takedown and put me through to Blur off the air.

"This is Blur. Is this Graham?" he asked.

"The one and only," I replied.

"Holy shit, you're a legend, son. The way you handed the globalists that defeat. Proud moment as a patriot. What can I help you with?" he asked.

"I'm running into a bit of a roadblock and I was hoping that you would be able to help me out with something. Have you ever heard of the Capstones to the Pyramids?" I asked.

The line was silent for a moment, which felt like an eternity. Finally, he spoke up.

"I can't get into this over the phone, but if you're willing to fly down here, I'll grab some dinner with you, and I'll tell you what I know. Let's say next Friday?"

"Yeah, that sounds fine. Can you give me the address and information I'll need," I said as he cut me off.

"My assistant will give it to you when I get off the phone. It's my personal cell phone and where our studio is located. Great talking to you, Graham. Never stop fighting the globalists!" he enthused, as he passed the call back to his assistant.

She gave me the information and I hung up. *God, he even acts like that off the air*, I thought. I wasn't sure if this was a good idea, but I'd come way too far to stop now. I passed out and, when I woke up, we were back in Boston. Jackson and I went online and spent $650 on tickets to Houston for our overnight trip. This was starting to get expensive; I wasn't sure how long I could keep it up. Little did I know that money was going to be the least of my concerns and that this was going to be the longest week of my life.

Chapter Four

We boarded the flight from BOS to IAH. Maybe it was a good thing that I had a week off, as I was able to put my questions together for Blur. I shot him a text from the plane letting him know we were on our way. He was a little apprehensive at first about Jackson coming with me, but I eventually persuaded him to be OK with it. What exactly does one do when they don't drink on a plane? I left my music player at home; I wanted to stay focused. My thoughts drifted towards Jackson briefly. This poor guy had no idea the kind of life he had gotten himself into. Sure, he might know what had happened previously, but was he really able to grasp it?

"How you feeling, Jax?" I asked him.

"Hanging in there, man," he replied.

Jackson wasn't much for flying or taking public transportation. He said he felt safer if he could control his surroundings. He downed a gin and tonic and ordered another. I wouldn't begrudge him that. It was my decision to get clean, and I wasn't about to impose it on anybody else.

Aside from some turbulence, the four-and-a-half-hour flight was basically uneventful. Half the time it took us to drive from Boston to DC. If I had unlimited money,

I'd fly everywhere. We had a car waiting for us at George Bush Airport, because there was no way I was going to deal with Jackson if he found out he had to take a cab.

It wasn't that bad a ride to Blur's studio on Clinton Drive. Oh, the irony. I wondered if he'd done that on purpose. His assistant was waiting for us at the door.

"Come on in," she said, in a soft southern twang.

We walked down a hallway toward his studio, turned the corner and there he was! Sitting behind his desk going into one of his rants. He looked over at us and, while still in character, handed the hosting duties over to Palau Towns, his charming British second-in-command, and made his way over to us.

"You made it," he said, enthusiastically.

"Yeah, we sure did. Are we heading out somewhere now or something?" I asked.

"I think we should just stay here. We've had some breaking news that I have to cover in a little bit, plus we just had pizza catered. Let's go to the kitchen and talk," he said.

We followed him back to a kitchen that looked like it was stuck in the '90s. We grabbed a slice each and sat.

"So, what's up, kid?" he asked.

"You know why we're here," Jackson replied.

"I do, but I want to hear it from you first," he said.

I took a deep breath.

"We need to know what you know about the missing Capstones of the Pyramids. One of the things we just got done doing was completely being shut out from the Masons' headquarters in DC. We even knew someone there, and he couldn't help us. Actually, he's the one that told us to come to you," I said.

"Of course, they're not going to tell you anything. This is above their pay grade, and he's not going to risk being excommunicated. Plus, they don't even really know the story. It's a no-fly zone. The only reason I know about this is because I did an undercover exposé on the 'Big Heaven Room' retreat that the elitists go to in California once a year, and one of the guests, I'm not going to say who, got too drunk and told me everything they knew," he said.

I was getting anxious with anticipation, but I was able to calm myself down. What the hell was the secret?

"OK, here goes," Blur said, as he opened the fridge and pulled out a tall boy of beer, cracked it and pounded half of it. He let out an enormous burp. I was starting to think this was not such a good idea.

"Thousands and thousands of years ago, the pyramids were built with sacred geometry and wisdom that we have lost over the ages. They had functions well above our understanding of current science, although no records were kept since they destroyed the library of

Alexandria," he said, taking another sip. "The story goes like this. When the Church was in its early stages and I mean infancy, people were sent to Cairo to study these monolithic beasts. What they reported back was disturbing and forever locked in the Vatican archives. A group of early priests removed the capstones to all three of the pyramids, and suddenly they lost their powers. This was done purposefully. Rumor has it that these three capstones were too sacred and important to be kept in one location, so they were scattered over the Earth. They are moved to new locations every time a new Pope is chosen, as a way to keep people from discovering the secret." He finished and took another huge gulp.

"What secret?" I asked, eyes wide.

"I have no idea. But supposedly there is another secret that is buried among the locations as well. One that could potentially have the power to destroy modern society. These are very powerful people we're talking about here, Graham, and the secrets they sit on could bring the entire operation down," he said.

"Why wouldn't they just keep them all in the Vatican archives, where they store all the Papal Bulls they've created?" I asked.

"Did you see what happened with the backlash to the Church when you exposed the Jesuits and the President with the secrets you uncovered? Did you see the protests outside the Vatican? Maybe they were thinking that in the event something like this ever happened and they were overrun, that they didn't want to have all their eggs in one basket?" He laughed. This guy was borderline crazy. But he was the only one giving answers, so I had to put up with it. "I've seen your videos that you've put online on AquaStream," he said.

Since I got a little more press coverage than a normal person should have gotten, I decided to start an AquaStream channel as TeddyGraham98, and create explanation videos about our previous adventure. I have about 220,000 subscribers. Combine that with the radio show and I'm the hottest D-list celebrity around. Truth be told, I only created that channel so that I could have a record of everything that has happened to me—to us—in the event that somebody tried to kill me.

"You're too popular for the globalists to just outright kill you, Graham, so you better be careful with your moves here." Blur finished his beer and went to the fridge to grab another.

"So how exactly are we supposed to find these capstones?" I asked.

"Did you know that it's been estimated that it would take $30 billion a year to eradicate world hunger? Is there any reason why the globalist elite shouldn't set an example by having the richest of the one percent take care of the first year? Plus, there are more boarded-up houses in the United States than there are homeless people. Seems to me, the answers are simple," he said.

Maybe he was catching a buzz and it was time to leave. "If you know where we can begin to find the first capstone, can you tell us?" I nudged.

He pounded the second beer and belched for about twelve seconds.

"Did you know there was a case where some reporters were hired to run a story about bovine growth hormone and the issues with it? Long story short, they did this story and were about to put it out, but Monsanto stepped in and tried to have them run an edited version that they provided. Fox TV's lawyers wanted them to as well. They refused and were going to report Fox to the FCC and were subsequently fired. So, they sued the station and won. But Fox appealed and it was overturned. The ruling? It's not illegal to falsify the news. This set a precedent for all news channels. We just try and report on stories the mainstream media doesn't touch, and they call us fake news and bash us every chance they get. Meanwhile, they're the ones distorting the truth and playing politics with major corporations. I hate them and I hate the globalists!" he finished.

"OK then, I think we'll be heading out. Thanks Blur," I said.

"Hold on a minute, Young Guns, I'm not done with you yet." He stood up and stretched. "I have no idea what will happen if the capstones, if they even exist, would do once they are put back in their rightful place. However, what I do know from that drunken fool at the Heaven event is that where they currently are is one land and two water locations. Supposedly the first one can be found having to do with climate change. Now get out of here and go kick some ass!" he said, excusing himself.

His assistant came back and walked us out. Damn it, Blur, I could have used a location. Well, what he provided would have to do for now. We got back in our rental car and headed back to the airport. I feel like we could have done this entire thing over WhatsApp or through Protonmail, a completely encrypted email system. This was a damn expensive trip and I was starting to run out of money. I had an idea of what I was going to do for capital but wasn't sure if it was going to work. No, it wasn't selling roses by the side of the road like Hannah suggested previously, and no, it wasn't porn either. I just needed to run it by everyone. This was going to be my last option and I was going to have to exercise it if I wanted to go anywhere.

Chapter Five

We got back to the house in Quincy after a too-long ride on the Red Line, which sucks, but trains are the same everywhere. I went to Long Island and New York City to visit some family a few years back and took the LIRR, and that sucked too. I walked through the door and the girls were waiting for us in their pajamas. Breakfast was made.

"Hi baby, find out anything interesting?" Hannah asked.

"A bunch of stuff, just nothing helpful at this exact moment. I still have no idea where to begin looking for this stuff," I said, sounding a little deflated.

"Hi Rider, did you enjoy yourself in Texas?" Rosette asked.

"Loved it, baby. Watched a chubby old dude pound beers and talk about some of the craziest shit I've ever heard in my entire life. Exactly what I wanted to do with my free time," he laughed.

"So how was Blur?" Hannah asked.

"He's exactly like he is on TV. He's always after the elitists. I honestly don't know how he hasn't been taken out yet," I said.

"He's too popular. It'd just deify him," Hannah said.

"So, what's the next plan, Stan?" Rosette asked.

"He said that there are one land and two water locations for the capstones right now. But he wasn't able to give us any information other than that the first one has to do with climate change. Also, what the hell is up with the Christ the Redeemer?" I asked.

"No clue. So that's it? End of the road?" Rosette asked.

"Not sure," I said, as I bit into an ostrich egg. The thing was huge, but I was starving. It suddenly dawned on me that humans could always be counted on to do one of two things when they discover something: find a way to eat it, or find a way to have sex with it.

"Remember the disappearing ink trick from earlier?" I asked, as I finished the egg.

"Of course," Hannah said.

"I'm running out of money here and I don't want to have to do this, but this is the last option," I said.

"Selling yourself?" Jackson asked.

"I don't think you understand. I went to raise my credit limit online and a fist came out of the screen and punched me in the dick," I replied.

"What the hell are you talking about, Newsdon?" Rosette asked.

"So, I went on free credit report dot com, and they told me I qualified for a Confederate flag," I said.

"Ha ha, can you please make some sense now, baby?" Hannah asked.

"I can't believe I'm going to do this, but I have to go up to Attleboro and make a visit. A visit to the person who sent me the encrypted letter to begin with," I said.

"And who would that be?" Rosette asked.

I took a deep breath and scanned the room. "Jean."

The room went dead silent as I started to pack my bags to go. I was going to have to do this alone. I hadn't seen him since everything went down and, to be honest, I had no idea how I'd react to seeing him. But if I wanted to continue this, I had to.

Chapter Six

I pulled up to the jail. I hadn't been inside a jail since getting caught drinking with a fake ID in undergrad. It was expunged because I did community service and promised the judge to never do it again. They give you a tour of the jail where massive inmates holler and throw urine at you, basically to scare the shit out of you.

I signed in and waited for my old friend Jean Solex to come out. After a few minutes, he appeared and looked thrilled to see me.

"You wrote the letter in lemon juice, didn't you?" I asked. "What the hell are you trying to start?"

"Mon ami, firstly you have to understand that I had no say in what happened to NP. I didn't realize that this was how things worked. If you're going to be elevated to a position of power, it requires a sacrifice of life to get you there. Ninety-nine percent of the time you don't have a say in it. It's either them or you. Sacrificing people has evolved over time. This is no different. If you saw the video, you'd see that I couldn't pull the trigger. Other arrangements were made. I know you think that I didn't like him, but that's not true at all. I also know that you may never forgive me and that's something I will have to learn to live with forever," he finished.

"It was completely unforgivable, and I know enough now to know that what you just said is right," I said. Truthfully, I had been studying what goes on at the Big Heaven Room. It's horrifying. Still, it was completely messed up that he went through with that.

"I don't expect to ever be friends again, but doing right by you is my raison d'etre now. I had to get your attention because it's something I overheard when I was in a place I wasn't supposed to be. I also couldn't risk writing it down in case someone ever found it. I'm glad you were able to figure it out. What do you know so far?"

"I know that I just spent nearly all my savings going to DC and Houston and all I learned was something about hypothetical capstones at water and land signs. Don't even know how to find them or what to do with them if I do. It's incredibly frustrating to not have my brilliant friend with me anymore. He'd know what to do," I said. I know that last part must have stung him a bit.

"I cannot apologize enough for that. I hope that one day you can forgive me. It was either his life or my life, and I made a choice. If I shot the teacher priest, they would have come after me and my whole family and burnt us to the ground. I will be making this up to you for the rest of my life. However, I am able to help in this aspect. I overheard someone, and I can't say who, say that the first capstone was moved to a location that's currently drawing a lot of attention because it has a climate change protest surrounding it. It's hidden in plain sight, so to speak."

He clammed up as one of the guards started moving closer.

"What are you saying? Do you have any more information than that?" I asked, but it was clear that our time was just about up.

"Look Graham, I know I messed up badly, and I know I can't stop apologizing for it, but I can make things easier for you. Rumor has it that if these are to be discovered or reunited with their rightful home, it would mark the end for many things as we know it."

He paused and looked over his shoulder. The guard was about eight feet away and slowly walking towards us.

"As you just mentioned, you just had your money depleted. I have an account that I keep as liquid assets. Has about $150,000 in it. It's yours," he said, handing me another blank piece of paper. "I have to go now. All I can say is that I overheard them say 'Hand to God'."

"Wait, tell me where it's located," I pleaded. But it was too late. The guard had already started to lead him away. I called out one more time, "Jean, please!" But he was being ferried away.

I turned around to leave and heard him shout my name before he went back in with the other inmates. I turned around and saw him make a heart with his hands above his head and tap his chest. He then disappeared into another room.

I left the jail and got back into the car. I sat there for a few minutes trying to wrap my head around what had just happened. I pulled out my phone and gave Hannah a call so that she'd know I was safe. I looked at the paper. It read, *Please forgive me.* If this wasn't the pits, I didn't know what was. Then something popped into my head.

Jean always dated but never settled down with anyone. But there was one girl that he used to talk about, Dominica from Italy. He said she was the one that got away. He always used to make that heart shape with his hands and thump his chest whenever she'd leave. She was a foreign exchange student in undergrad at Georgetown and went back after a year. I hadn't thought about her in years. Where the hell was she from, though? I couldn't remember and it was going to drive me insane.

I fiddled around with my phone, looking at a map of Italy to see if anything jogged my memory. Nothing. God, this was frustrating. I dropped my keys on the floor and couldn't find them. It was getting dark and I turned on my phone's flashlight to locate my keys. I was still holding onto that piece of paper. Of course!

Unfortunately, the light in the car wasn't going to cut it, so I popped the trunk. I had gone camping not too long ago and had a lantern there. I turned it on and waited a few minutes. All at once a note appeared under the words 'forgive me.' It showed his banking information and passwords to the vault. Then taking up half the page was the word 'Venice.' Yes, that was it! That was where she was from. And apparently where I was going.

Chapter Seven

I got back to the house shortly after ten PM. I expected everyone to be sleeping at that point, but they were all awake watching TV. Hannah wasted no time trying to find out what happened.

"How's your ass feeling, baby?" she asked.

"I'll survive," I said. Of course, she went there.

"What did you end up finding out?" Rosette asked.

"A few things, actually. Well, first of all, he explained why he did what he did. The sad thing is that I almost feel for him because I know what an impossible situation it was for him to be in," I said, knowing that Rosette would pipe up.

"He's a piece of shit, Graham. There's a fair to middling chance NP would still be alive," she said.

I got where she was coming from. Not in the sense that their relationship would have changed, even though she took it hard when he was killed and was overly sensitive about her relationship with him. She also really loved Jackson. But I got it.

"You're right Rosette, there's no excusing that," I replied. "But you have to understand that he gave me this." I showed them the piece of paper.

"What in the sweet buttery Jesus is that?" Rosette asked.

"His secret bank account. He gave me access to it as well as the code to his vault. Money's not a problem anymore. He also told me where we were going first. Have any of you ever been to Venice?"

"Even if the capstone thing is true, how are we to know that he's telling the truth about this now?" Hannah asked.

"We don't. We just have to trust him. He's the one that pointed us in this direction to begin with. It doesn't make much sense for him to lead us astray after introducing us to this craziness. Also, I cannot emphasize enough how remorseful he was for what had happened. Like I said, I almost feel bad for him. The only thing we need to figure out is where in Venice we are going. All I know is that we're going somewhere where there is a climate change demonstration or something like that," I tailed off.

"Let's Google it." Rosette whipped her phone out and started scrolling through it. "OK, so I see that years ago there were protests in Venice due to climate change and the upcoming Paris conference. They protested before the G7 summit in Bologna," she said, furrowing her brow. "OK, so basically Venice is sinking. We're watching a modern day sunken city be born," she finished.

"This doesn't help us figure out where we have to go," Hannah said.

"I know, I'm trying here. I need you to give me something more," she replied.

"I have to tell you something, Graham," Jackson said. "In physics, the 'Big Bang Theory' states that everything that ever existed, was singularity. And then exploded, spreading outward since the beginning of time. For many years, the entire world thought that this was the beginning. There's a new theory called the 'Big Crunch' that says the universe expands and then contracts and everything will eventually condense back to singularity again, starting the Big Bang Theory cycle all over again. There's no way of telling how many eons the expansion and constriction goes. We've been trying to figure out what to do and where to go with this information."

Jackson's a major nerd. He finds a way to bring physics into every conversation if he can. The only way to fight this is by being ridiculous or offensive.

"Jackson, while I appreciate the information, when you go off on these tirades, you make me want to strip naked and rub myself with hemlock from head to toe," I said.

"Ooh, did you know that in the 19th century, they used to douse tampons in belladonna to relieve period cramps?" Rosette added.

"Can you dumbasses stop talking about poisonous plants for two seconds and try and figure out what our next step should be?" Hannah interjected.

"Right, sorry. He did mention one other thing. He said something about a Hand to God," I added.

"A what?" Rosette said.

"Exactly what I said. A Hand to God."

"I'm going to look that up right now," Rosette said.

I shot a look at my girlfriend and realized how lucky I was that she had put up with me all that time before. I was always a few drinks deep and she never said a word to me. We've only gotten stronger since I stopped. Life was good and that was for damn sure. After a few minutes, Rosette spoke up.

"So *Hand to God* was an Off-Broadway play written years ago. It took place in a religious town of Cypress in Texas. Had something to do with puppets and avoiding Satan," she kept reading. "I don't think this has anything to do with it," she finished.

"Back to the beginning," I said.

"People have God all wrong," Jackson said.

"What?" I replied.

"Think about it. So, string theory in physics states that there is room for eleven dimensions. We are currently in the third dimension, fourth if you count time. We have no idea what dark matter, excuse me, dark energy *is*, even though it's the majority of space. That's just our dimension. R. Buckminster Fuller said, 'Since the initial publication of the chart of the electromagnetic spectrum, humans have learned that what they can touch, smell, see and hear is less than one-millionth of reality.' If there are 11 dimensions, and remember, this is as far as we've gotten so far in physics . . . and we don't even know our own dimension, how can we begin to understand a being that has created other dimensions we have yet to understand? We know these dimensions exist because the Hadron collider produced the Higgs-Boson particle that popped into our dimension, something also known as the 'God particle,' " he said.

"You know what I don't get? I don't understand how I don't pay my taxes and they immediately try to foreclose my house. But then you pick up a newspaper and read about Susan who has been dead for 45 years in her New York City condo, and nobody came to check on her," I replied with absolute nonsense.

"My point is, Graham, how can we begin to understand a divine being when we don't even understand our own reality?" he asked.

"I'm sure this isn't the *Hand to God* we're trying to figure out, but it's good information to store inside my brain. I hope it didn't push out anything important," I smiled.

"First of all, Newsdon," Rosette began, "you haven't figured out that you're just proving the cobra effect with your answers to him?" she said.

As a psych student, she also spoke in terms of her field. The cobra effect occurs when an attempted solution to a problem—Jackson's physics tirades and my replies—make the problem worse, by enabling him further. I don't care. It's funny.

We sat around for a few more minutes. My mind started drifting to NP. He was just so freaking smart and he would have figured out what to do by now. I thought back to the last doodle I saw on his desk when we went to his apartment and were accosted by the cops. 'He determines the number of the stars and calls them each by name: Psalm 147:4'. So true. But it's not helping with the problem we're having now.

"Oh my God, I think I found something," Rosette squealed.

"What is it?" Hannah replied.

"There was a sculpture in Venice years ago that was taken down, but recently put back up because it apparently agrees with people. It looks like a giant set of hands reaching out of the canals. It was also created in response to climate change. This has something to do with rising water levels in Venice," she said, showing us a picture.

This has to be it, I thought. *This has to be where the first capstone is located. The only problem is, if there's a ginormous capstone in the water, how are we going to recover it, remove it and take it away without being seen?* I had some time to think about this as I began looking for a flight. Thank you, Jean, for your kind contribution to our quest. Little did we know that once we were in Venice, we would wake a sleeping giant who was already all too eager to take us out.

Chapter Eight

"Woo-hoo! We're going to Italy!" Rosette squealed.

"Calm down sister, we have a lot to do before we get there," I said. This was true. We had to get plane tickets and hotel rooms. We also had to locate a scuba suit as I was pretty sure people would not like me diving into the water in plain view. Also, once we got to Venice, we were going to have to scope the area out and figure out the best way to do this. My head hurt just thinking about it all.

"OK, I'll look up the plane and hotel and you figure out the rest, Newsdon," Rosette said.

We spent the next few hours making flight arrangements for our little trip. Seventeen hundred dollars per person, thirteen-hour flight and we had to transfer in Toronto for some reason. We were also able to find a late night dive store in Boston that was willing to sell us a full suit with oxygen for eight hundred bucks. Thanks for everything, Jean. Rosette and Jackson went back to Chestnut Hill to pack and pick up the scuba gear. We were going to need an extra suitcase just for it. Our flight was the next morning. It was the best we could do on such short notice.

"Anything you want to talk about, baby?" she asked, as she began packing.

"I'm just wondering. What if this is all bullshit? What if this is like that movie *Contact* where they went through an elaborate ruse to chase something and it turned out that nothing happened at all?" God bless this woman who puts up with references to movies she's never seen.

"It's not like we're paying for this," she said. "What really gets to me is that Jean went through all this and maybe it's for a joke. But why would he be willing to pay for all of this?" she asked.

She had a valid point. The truth was, until I got to the hotel to see if there was anything in the water under the sculpture, I had no idea if this was real or fake. I started packing my stuff, realizing that what we were about to do was not only dangerous, but highly illegal. If there was a giant pyramid stone down there, how was I supposed to move it?

Blur Slanders was on TV talking about another conspiracy of his. I didn't pay attention. I was too preoccupied with my own thoughts, like, what if I end up in an Italian jail or worse, murdered by the Illuminati? The return flight to Logan was two days after our arrival and didn't leave us much time to get things done. *God, I wish*

James was still around. He would tell us how to avoid detection.

NP would have also known exactly what to do and what to avoid. I'm still not over losing them. It's not even getting any easier. I don't know if I'll ever be able to have a day where my thoughts are not consumed by those two. I've been having trouble sleeping at night and more often than not, I dream about them. I hope they're at peace wherever they are.

My thoughts turned back to Hannah as she finished packing. I still couldn't believe that after everything we'd been through in the last year or so, she could be so casual about it all. Either she really loved me, or she was just as crazy as I am. I also wondered about Jackson, and how calm he was about finding out everything that we'd come to learn. He did seem like an adrenaline junkie though, something I picked up on when I heard about all the Tough Mudder races he'd done. Before my mind could turn to another thing, we got a phone call from Rosette.

"Newsdon, we're packed and ready to go. We picked up your wet suit. It's freaking heavy. Anyways we picked you both up some Nyquil for tonight and the plane ride tomorrow. Can you leave the door unlocked?"

"Of course, baby girl," I said. "How far out are you?"

"Twenty minutes. We picked up dinner. We haven't eaten all day and we're starving. Make sure you're awake when we get there," she said, before hanging up.

I took a break from packing and sat down to watch some Blur. He was talking about some woman named 'Svali,' who apparently used to be an Illuminati mind control programmer, but broke free and gave a bunch of interviews about it. Until she was silenced, and the interviews abruptly stopped. I Googled it and it turned out that there were interviews from a lady who claimed just that. Her name also matched. It was amazing how much material this guy managed to get through every day.

I returned to something I was thinking about earlier. The Four Horsemen of the Bible were just the four Sagittarius. Four gospels and since the son/sun dies in Sagittarius then these four would represent the death in each gospel. I then started to wonder if the Chinese Zodiac played a part in their culture and special books.

"Thanks for bringing the food," Jackson said.

"Sorry, I was in my own world. Can I see the suit?" I replied.

"It's in the car. Go look," Rosette said.

I went outside to get it out of the car. They weren't kidding, it was heavy. I took it inside so I could try it on. It fit perfectly. I went into the living room to get everyone's reactions.

"Nice suit baby, you look hot," Hannah cooed.

"Shut up, Husker. You look like you're the star of a fetish website," Rosette injected.

"I can barely hear you with this on," I said. "What do you think, Jackson?"

"Weren't you on Spongebob last week?" he laughed.

"Screw you guys." I changed into pajamas and joined everyone for some dinner and R&R. We had a great time, and everyone went to bed by ten o'clock. We had a mid-day flight the next day and were going to be exhausted. I thanked Rosette for the Nyquil but didn't even touch the stuff because of the alcohol in it. It was nice to have everyone around relaxing, despite what we had to do. If I had known what we were about to get into, I would have told everyone to stay home. The chain of events that would come would soon endanger all of our lives.

You are not a physical being that's evolved a consciousness, you are a conscious being that's evolved a physical experience. - The Prodigy2186 (Internet Personality)

Chapter Nine

We touched down at Marco Polo airport mid-afternoon. That gave us plenty of time to get to Hotel Persaro Palace, which was only a few blocks away from the canal. The plan was to wait until nightfall, then scope out the Ca d'ora which is where I planned on sliding into the water. It sucks when you have to plan your highly illegal, dangerous expeditions using Google Maps, but that's what we had to do. We hunkered down in our hotel suite and went over the plan.

"So, what's the deal? Are you planning to wear your frog suit in public or do you have other plans?" Jackson asked.

"Is he going to strip down butt naked and put the suit on in the street?" Rosette retorted.

"Take it easy guys, there's plenty of me to go around," I laughed.

"Very funny, Newsdon. We do need to figure this shit out, though," she said.

"Well it's a good thing we're doing this tomorrow. Tonight is just a test run. So, let's go out, have a drink, and scope the area out," I suggested.

We unpacked and headed down to the bar of this establishment's fine restaurant. I ordered Pellegrino. The rest of the team ordered various drinks to calm their nerves. The sun finally started to set after an hour at the bar . . . the eternal battle between the Egyptian Gods Horus and Set.

Horus was born on December 25 to a virgin and was known to fight the Egyptian God, Set. In Egyptian mythology, Horus represents the Sun. So, when people ask what hour it is, they're really asking the location of Horus (the Sun) in the sky. Horus and "hours" are just anagrams of one another.

We waited another half hour after sunset to make sure it was dark. It was important to duplicate the results tomorrow.

We made our way to the Ca d'ora. It was a beautiful walk through a city much older than ones we're used to in the States.

We arrived at Ca d'ora and quickly found a bathroom in a restaurant nearby. If we were going to have dinner, this restaurant looked like the kind of place someone on *The Bachelor* would take one of his girls to. I finished up and met the team by the wharf.

"OK, so this is it guys. This is where it all goes down tomorrow," Hannah said.

We searched the surrounding area and made note of everything we saw. There were people walking around but most of them were either drunk or disinterested in what was going on around them. We found a secluded area near the wharf. Perfect! I checked the parameters. No one seemed to notice. This is where I decided to enter the murky depths of the water. Now, the tricky part.

We walked down the street alongside the water, trying to get to the Ca Sagredo hotel. Navigating underwater was going to be a bitch, but it was a straightforward walk. We arrived at the hotel and immediately noticed a giant pair of hands sticking out of the water, as if holding the building up. They were awe-inspiring. I couldn't believe the locals considered taking them down.

"Those are some big-ass hands," Jackson said, observant as ever.

"If what Jean said is right, there's a treasure among treasures under it," I replied, wondering how big the stone would be. The great pyramids are enormous. Yet we still don't know how they were built. Sure, there were videos on AquaStream showing how technology might have allowed the ancient Egyptians to manipulate heavy objects, and people who used lever and pulley systems that could do the same, but the sheer size was outrageous.

What if it was too big to carry? What if it was too big to even move? What if it had a security system around it?

"Hey guys, I'm worried about getting from point A to B in possibly pitch-black water. Any ideas?" I asked.

"Rose and I were just talking about that, sweetie. We came up with a good one. We're going to take a Gondola ride right before you slip in and have them take us in a loop from Ca d'ora to the hotel. Maybe a little further and then turn around. Just follow us from under there," Hannah said.

This was a brilliant idea. I had no idea how long oxygen tanks lasted and wasn't sure if I could see them above me. But following a slow boat sounded like a good idea.

"OK, sounds like a plan. Now let's go out and have some fun. We work at night, no need to go to bed early," I said.

We went back to the L'alcova restaurant where I was earlier and had a few rounds of appetizers and they had a few drinks. *Man, if only I could have a few drinks, I'd feel better about tomorrow. The thought of an Italian jail cell is just freaking me out.* Then I remembered that I can't just have a few drinks, I have to take it all the way when I do. I sipped on my Orangina, which blew the American version out of the water. We sat and talked about everything that we had learned in the last year.

Having Jackson around, I felt like I had a bodyguard I never knew I needed. Little did we know, however, that tomorrow was not going to go exactly as planned and we were going to have to do some quick thinking to make it out of Italy in one piece.

"Great minds discuss ideas, average minds discuss events, small minds discuss people." - Eleanor Roosevelt

Chapter Ten

We arrived at the dock at approximately nine PM. The sun had already set, and the city had a cool majestic glow around it. We went to our secret location and waited for the last couple to leave the area. I dropped down a few steps and quickly unzipped the duffel bag carrying the suit and oxygen tank. My friends formed a barrier around me as I changed. Jackson alone should have been enough to block me, I can't stress enough how jacked the guy is.

"Well, here goes nothing. Any final words before we get this show on the road?" I asked.

"Did you know corn flakes were created as a cure for masturbation?" Rosette asked.

"Did you know that a pig's orgasm can last up to 30 minutes?" Hannah interjected.

"I love bacon," Jackson added.

"Guys, I'm serious. Can we go over the plan one more time?" I asked.

We went over the plan again. I was supposed to swim to the Ca Segrado and bring whatever I found back to the secluded area. We brought a blanket that was large enough to cover, well, who knows . . . This had disaster written all over it. When we'd walked from this area to the hotel the night before, we'd counted the steps, which was supposed to help me know exactly where I was in the water.

"Alright, see you on the other side," I said, back-flipping into the canal. The first thing I noticed in its murky depths was how pitch black it was. It also smelled like shit . . . the smell made me want to retch. I would need to be hosed down CDC style when I got out.

I floated along, timing my kicks as if I were taking steps. This was going to take longer than I thought. I also wasn't sure if I had enough oxygen but couldn't come out of the water for fear of being seen. Panic crept up my spine and goosebumps rose on my arms. I made the decision to raise myself a little higher in the water. Still pitch black, and still nothing. I checked my oxygen and I was down to a quarter tank. How was that even possible? I was starting to panic.

So, there I was, surrounded by a sea of black, my oxygen running out. I was about to give up when I looked above and saw the boat just a few feet above my head, its oars going in and out of the water. Finally! I had no idea where they found a gondola this late at night. I stayed a few feet back, away from the oars. After five more minutes at this slow and romantic pace I crept to the surface as quietly as I could. I could see the hands and a pool of light surrounding them about a thousand feet ahead of me. I followed the boat until I arrived at the hands and dove all the way down. My oxygen was down to 15%. I was going to have to find this thing and haul ass back to the surface. As I was carefully kicking my way down to the bottom, trying not to disturb the water, I was thinking this thing was going to bring us to the land of 'milk and honey.'

Symbolically, milk, of course, represented the Milky Way Galaxy. The center of the Milky Way is Sagittarius, which is also where the Sun of God dies. The honey represents the 'Beehive Cluster' asterism in Cancer, where the Sun is at its throne on June 21. I realized that they were opposing signs at their cusp. The story of the rise and the fall of God's Sun again. According to Blur Slanders, the Illuminati is heavily influenced by bees.

I dove to the bottom, which really wasn't that far at all, which I learned after smacking my head on something hard and nearly dislodging my mask. That would have been bad. I saw a dark outline and tried to make out what it was. I wished I were colorblind. It sounds crazy, but colorblind people can see better in the dark.

I checked my oxygen—12%. I had to make a decision. It appeared to be a sort of chest. I grabbed it by the handles and picked it up. It was surprisingly light considering its size. As I lifted the chest, I noticed a flash of light, but it disappeared shortly after I pulled it away. I turned around and kicked as fast as my flippers could take me. I knew where I was going, I just had to make it back. I checked my oxygen again. I was down to 8%. This was going to be a photo finish. It occurred to me that even if I made it back, where was my crew? Did they take the gondola back? I didn't see it. *God, I hope I don't surface and they're still walking back.*

I made it back with 4% oxygen left in my tank. I poked my head out of the water and saw my clothes a few feet away, undisturbed on a blanket. I verified that no one else was around and dragged the chest out of the water, quickly throwing the blanket over it. A few feet away, I changed back into my regular clothes in the darkness and tossed the SCUBA suit and the oxygen tank into the water. Good riddance. I smelled like a septic tank.

I sat on the chest for about fifteen minutes until I saw the team approaching out of the corner of my eye. Their eyes lit up when they saw me.

"So, what did you find?" Jackson asked.

"I was too scared to take a close look, it's under this blanket. Let's carry it back to the hotel. I need a shower," I said.

Jackson and I carried the chest to the hotel, where I promptly excused myself and jumped into the shower. When I returned, they all had puzzled looks on their faces.

"What's up, guys?" I asked, as puzzled as they were.

"You need to take a look at this thing," Rosette said.

I sat on the bed and looked inside. It reminded me of a treasure chest, but not . . . there was a screen inside with some sort of film covering it. I peeled it off, and the screen came to life. I wasn't sure if the film had been protecting it from water damage, but I had managed to activate it somehow. There was an electronic keypad, with a four-digit number written on it. There was also something etched on top that I couldn't make out. I got a little bit closer and read it.

During the Age of the Ram, there was life and some experienced double life. Those with the understanding can continue.

What could this possibly mean? "Any idea what this refers to?" I asked.

"Well, it has to be the code to unlock this thing," Hannah said.

"Well the age of the Ram was Aries, and that was 2308-148 BC," I said.

"Yeah, but that's not set in stone. A number of astrotheologists claim each sign is 2000 years instead of 2160 years. There's debate as to when the age begins and ends. Even if you get through all of that, the calendars are all screwed up. None of them agree on anything," Hannah said.

"Yeah, the Chinese calendar is ahead of us in year 4100 and change. Their New Year isn't the same, either," Jackson said.

"Did you know that the Ethiopian calendar is thirteen months long? It's twelve 30-day months and then one additional month of 5 days. They also celebrate New Year's on September 11. Which is super morbid for us if you think about it," I added.

"The Hebrew calendar is almost in year 6000. They don't even have a leap day every four years like the Gregorian Calendar, they have a leap month. Their New Year is also in September," Rosette said.

"How did you know that, Rose?" I asked.

"I dated this Jewish guy a few years back," she said. "He kept trying to explain his religion and all this mysticism. Honestly, it just wasn't my thing."

"Actually wait, that kind of does help a bit. The age of the Ram was the Jewish golden years," I recalled, thinking back to when NP taught us about the ram's horn and why they blew it on the holidays. It was still hard to think about NP, even in situations like this. He would definitely know what to do next.

We stared at the box for what seemed like an eternity. I had never seen a contraption like this. None of us dared to enter a pass code unless we were sure of it. For all we knew, it could explode and kill us all.

We decided to go downstairs and eat while we cleared our minds. I wasn't hungry, but the other three were starving. We sat down and everybody ordered a drink, and I got myself a Fanta Zero.

"So Rose, when did you date that Jewish kid? What was his name?" I asked. I was shocked I had never heard of him.

"Jesse. It was for only a month and a half in the summer between your undergrad and med school. He was . . ." Her voice trailed off, and she had this super focused look on her face.

We sat there in silence for a minute, trying to give her room to think when she suddenly picked up her drink and pounded it.

"I know what that code is," she said.

We took the food back to the room, where she sat us all down. "I know this is going to sound crazy, but I'm pretty sure I know what this code is," she continued. "It jogged my memory when we were all taking about New Year's dates."

"I also forgot to mention the reason that our New Year's date is January 1 at midnight and not December, March, June, September 21, the solstices or the equinoxes, which would make more sense Zodiactically. It's because our dog star, Sirius, is as high as it gets, directly above our heads, then directly under it is the Earth, and then directly under the Earth is the Sun. It's a perfect alignment. Only happens one day a year," I finished.

"Interesting, but are you done interrupting, Newsdon?" she asked.

"Yes sorry," I said.

"Anyways we started talking about New Year's dates, and then I brought up the Jewish thing, and then I told you about Jesse. One of the things Jesse used to talk about was something called Gematria. This is the practice of assigning numerical value to a letter. So, in English the letter A would be 1, B would be 2 and so on and so forth. There's a thing that Jewish people wear around their neck called 'Chai' that's supposed to be for good luck. It means 'life.' Its numerical value is 18. 'There was life and double life,' " she trailed off and turned her attention to the box. She punched in the code 1836. The box beeped twice and unlocked. The grin on her face was priceless.

"Well done, girl," Hannah said.

I leapt up and opened the box. In it was a rolled-up parchment, and under that was a cloth like the shroud of Turin. We carefully removed it, and there in front of us, to everyone's shock was one of the capstones. It was black and made of material that I couldn't place. It didn't look like it was from Earth. I lifted it up, shocked by how small it was. It was dense and heavy with a shiny glow. It also had a hole at its peak. I wrapped it back up and took it across the room and put it in my suitcase. Our work was done here. I went back to the chest and opened the parchment from its plastic casing. Another ominous message:

By the Hand of God discovered in the language of the people of Aries, so shall the second one be in the following sign of Pisces. The ruling planet stood vigilant and kept watch over it until it was brought down in the last days of the rooster at the hands of the Scorpion towards the last days of the Fish. It remains a shadow of its former self, yet ever vigilant as its guard. The second secret comes from the one who calls this place his birthplace yet bore a terrible secret.

We sat there for a few minutes and nobody had any brilliant ideas. We decided to call it quits for the night as we had a flight in the morning back to the States. Little did I know that the flash of light I saw in the water as well as my careless disregarding of the SCUBA suit was going to have dire consequences for us. Something was brewing up in the Vatican, we just didn't know it yet.

As above so below – Emerald Tablets from Hermes

Chapter Eleven

Pope Ignatius I sat back in his chair as he watched the College of Cardinals depart after their latest meeting. He was feeling a bit old and tired as of late. In truth, he had been feeling tired for quite a while now. There had been so many scandals within the Church that he was having a hard time keeping up a positive attitude. The pedophile scandal that had brought down the previous pope and put him in power was still going on, and the public's view of him was none too kindly. He wondered how long it would be before he would have to step down. This was not what he had hoped to accomplish when he was elected to the papacy. As the first Jesuit pope elevated to his stature, he took the name Ignatius after Loyola who began the Society of Jesus and held strong to its tenements.

He wanted to change the world, but he couldn't get half of the cardinals on board with him for major decisions. There was also that scandal from that boy from the United States who unraveled a complicated story that he was not initially aware of, but eventually found to be true. He had been speaking with Aurelio Celso, head of the Society of Jesus, also known as the Black Pope, regarding this. There were some who believed this kid should be taken out before he had time to do any more damage. After all, he did have quite a following on AquaStream. As he sat and watched the cardinals depart, the Camerlengo, Jean-Louis, came running in.

"Your Holiness, we need to talk," Jean-Louis said.

"Can this wait? This has been a trying day for me so far," Ignatius replied.

"It can't, I'm sorry. The first capstone has been removed," he exhaled.

"What? When?"

"Late last night. The camera sensor snapped a picture, but it was someone in a scuba suit, so we weren't able to capture a face. Here look," Jean-Louis said as he handed the Pope the picture.

Pope Ignatius slumped in his chair. There it was, clear as day, a person in a scuba suit removing the chest. He had feared this day for his entire papacy. As was tradition, every time a new Pope is elected, they rearranged these treasure chests around the world, leaving only cryptic messages as to how to find the new ones. They felt that these were too valuable to keep in the Vatican vault, and the way things were going these days within the Church and their 'extracurricular' activities, he was surprised there wasn't a restless movement to break into the vault.

"I have feared this day for a long time," he said to the Camerlengo.

"What should we do?" Jean-Louis pleaded.

"We have to do our homework, and look into it," Aurelio Celso said, inviting himself into the conversation. "Your Holiness, I've called back the cardinals, we need to address this now."

A few minutes later, the room was full of the College of Cardinals again. The Pope and the Camerlengo sat while Aurelio addressed the council.

"Gentlemen. Something pressing has come up. It seems that the first capstone has been removed," he said, as the cardinals began to murmur. "I don't need to remind you how crucial it is to what we are trying to accomplish that this ends here," he finished.

"When was this done?" one cardinal asked.

"Late last night. The camera caught a picture of the person who discovered this and removed it, but he was in a full scuba suit. There is no further information on that, other than he seemed to have been swimming away from the hotel," he finished.

"Your Holiness, what do you think we should do?" another cardinal shouted.

Pope Ignatius took a long hard minute to think before he answered.

"It is true that this has the potential to bring down everything, but there is a chance this could be a one-off event. Although this person did take the chest, there's a great chance they will not be able to open it. Perhaps he or she will put it back," he replied. In a strange way, he almost felt that this was a good thing for the Church. If this ever came out, they would be able to start from scratch and rebuild it stronger. The secret they were hiding was starting to become too much to manage.

"Your Holiness, I along with most of the cardinals here will have to strongly disagree with your point. You know very well what this contains, and it cannot be allowed to see the light of day," Aurelio said. There were nods and agreement in the background.

"What would you suggest we do, Aurelio?" Ignatius said.

"It's already done. I'm heading over to Venice to investigate the area and see what I can find," Silvio said, as he entered the room.

Silvio Bruno was a former Swiss Guard turned jack-of-all-trades. There were even rumors he was an assassin. Pope Ignatius remembered him rising up the ranks when he was still in the Society of Jesus, well before Aurelio took over. This man only made his face known when something serious was about to happen. He had been the one to neutralize those who got too close to Church secrets.

He remembered when he had first heard about Bruno. There was a journalist who supposedly came to Vatican City to take pictures of the 'Court of the Pine Cone.' He wrote an article stating that the pine cone could be found throughout history in statues and paintings and that it represented the pineal gland in the brain, or the third eye. This is also why Hindus put a dot in the middle of their forehead, because it represents it and that is where it's located. He also talked about how the pine cones were flanked by two birds which were phoenixes, referring to the story of the birth and death and eventual coming back to life. Even the Pope had a staff that had a pine cone on it. He began to make more connections about how the Church was hiding other secrets in plain sight, until one day his apartment burned to the ground. Nothing was ever heard from him again.

Pope Ignatius had once asked him if he felt uncomfortable working in the Vatican with a last name like Bruno, referring of course to Giordano Bruno, a scientist who was killed for his beliefs and rejection of Catholicism. Silvio had just turned to him and smiled and said, "I'm over it."

"I leave in an hour," Silvio said as he turned and walked out, suitcase behind him.

The Pope sat and thought a bit about what had just happened. He was angry that Aurelio had gone behind his back and set this up, but at the same time he was well aware that most of the cardinals no longer agreed with him and his viewpoints. They found Aurelio to be re-freshing and a go-getter.

"I will keep you all apprised of the status. Thank you everyone," the Pope said. The cardinals started talking among themselves as they slowly left the room. Only the Camerlengo and the Black Pope remained.

"You don't think this is just going to draw attention to this situation?" the Pope asked Aurelio.

"Whether it does or does not is irrelevant. This is something that cannot be allowed to see the light of day. And I am willing to go to any length to make sure that it stays hidden from the world," he replied.

The Camerlengo was confused. He knew about the chests, but he did not know what they contained or what they were to be used for. The way everyone was talking about them made them seem supernatural.

"I agree it shouldn't come to light, but perhaps when we find out who this person is, we can just bring them here and have a discussion with them. Cut it off before it gets any worse. Truth is, they won't be able to know what this is without collecting all three," the Pope said to a half-confused audience.

"This is where you and I differ, Your Holiness. There is nothing greater than this secret. I will do whatever I have to, to keep it a secret," Aurelio said and turned to leave.

The Camerlengo watched Aurelio walk out the door and shake hands with the cardinals. Politics as usual. The Camerlengo worried for Pope Ignatius. He had always treated him fairly and helped him into the position that he now found himself in.

"I have to say, Jean-Louis, I am worried about the future of our great Church. It seems it's always division and politics. Everyone used to be on the same page. I'm just worried that Silvio could end up drawing attention to this," he said.

"Your Holiness, I must ask, what is this big secret everybody is trying to keep quiet?" Jean-Louis asked.

The Pope took a deep breath and realized that if he explained this to Jean-Louis, he could be a wildcard and possibly expendable. The cardinals knew about the treasure chests that contained secrets, but they did not know what he knew. What the Black Pope knew. He knew he could never tell the Camerlengo out of love for him, it would just make him a target. This was drawing a wedge between the cardinals and himself, and Aurelio was more than happy to play devil's advocate. There were times that he felt he was not going to be Pope much longer. He felt a mutiny within the ranks and at times worried for his life. However, little did anybody know, but the Pope went on a two-week trip before he was elected and came up with an extremely elaborate failsafe to make sure that if anything ever happened to him, this secret would be discovered. A secret bigger than the Vatican hiding the existence of Pope Joan, the first female pope.

Chapter Twelve

Silvio Bruno hopped into his rental car and made the six-hour drive to Venice in four hours and 50 minutes. He lived for this adrenaline rush. Not just a "fast cars" rush, but a rush from doing something much bigger than himself. He parked his car at the Ca Sagredo Hotel and got out and looked around. It was early evening and he would only have to wait a short while before he could dive into the water and see what he found.

He noticed the big hands on the wall and wondered why someone would hide something so precious where so many people were around. He understood the idea of hiding clues or valuables in plain sight but thought this was too risky. It's amazing that it had taken this long for someone to snatch it from right under their noses.

He thought back to Aurelio and all that he'd done to groom him for the position that he was in right now. Aurelio was arguably the most powerful person under the Church's radar. Few people outside of his immediate circle even knew he existed, much less what he was capable of. He liked it that way.

He walked down the street, taking in all the sights and planning his escapade. He took note of where people were aggregating the most, the gondola rides, the bridges and the underpasses. He walked for fifteen minutes before coming across a restaurant. He stepped inside to use the bathroom and order a seltzer. While he was at the urinal, he wondered if the person who had taken the chest had been in the same restaurant a day before, enjoying drinks. He went up to the bartender and asked if there were any unusual customers there the night before. The bartender shook his head. Even if they were, he told him, they don't have a camera system. *Shit*, Silvio thought.

He sat down, slowly sipping club soda until the sun went down. Afterwards, he returned to the car. There were far fewer people around. He took his suitcase and entered the hotel, where he checked into the room closest to the entrance. There was a large party in the next room, possibly a wedding, he thought. Too many people around. He had to be careful not to be seen when he left the hotel.

He called Aurelio and told him he had arrived and started doing recon on the area and would check back in with him if anything turned up. He then opened his suitcase, took his clothes off, and carefully folded them into a waterproof carryon bag. He changed into his own scuba suit and oxygen tank, covering himself with a giant robe. He carried the mask under his arm, hiding it under the robe as he slunk to a dark deserted corner. He disrobed, tossing the robe into a nearby dumpster before slipping into the water and slowly swam around the corner in the dank unlit water. He wasn't sure what he was looking for exactly, as he had never seen the secret location to begin with. He eventually looked up, noticing the giant white hands and positioning himself between them. He immediately saw that the ground had recently been disturbed. There was also an extremely thin wire nearby. He plucked it and a camera rose from beneath the sand and snapped a picture of him, blinding him with the flash. *The tripwire must have been set to keep the chest in place*, he thought, struggling to see again, after the blinding flash.

He turned around and swam back to the area he had scoped out earlier, hoping to find something in the water. The canal wasn't very wide, so he would notice if anything was out of place. He did notice the pungent odor of the water though. Despite being an assassin who was used to blood, he prided himself on keeping clean at all times. He slowly swam down the canal, looking left and right. The water was getting darker, so he turned on the light on his helmet and dove even deeper, careful that people above would not notice what was going on below. So far, nothing.

He kept swimming and looking around and was beginning to lose hope until he saw something bunched up under the overpass ahead. He turned his light off and crept to the surface to see where he was, sticking his head out of the water as quietly as he could. Nobody was around to notice him, but he saw that he was at the overpass near the restaurant he had visited. He descended again and swam to a mass that seemed to have gotten snagged on a log. He tried to see what it was, but it was too dark.

He grabbed it and surfaced under the bridge. He quickly opened his waterproof bag and changed out of the wet suit and into his street clothes. He then carefully slid his scuba suit back into the water. Finally, he looked down at what he had retrieved from the water and was taken aback. It was a wet suit with an oxygen tank! *Someone must have had the same idea I had*, he thought. He put the wet suit and the oxygen tank into his bag and zipped it up, and carefully climbed to the surface of the bridge without anyone noticing him, looking around to see if there were any cameras facing the water. What would he do if he had just uncovered a secret and needed to get out of the street with a chest?

He looked to his left and squinted. There was a hotel not far away. He walked over and went inside. He asked the clerk if he had seen anything out of the ordinary the night before. When the man refused to answer, Silvio rolled his eyes and took out his expired Swiss Guard ID. The clerk went to get the manager.

After a minute, Silvio decided to have a cigarette. Outside, he noticed a rather large dumpster and thought, *What the hell, maybe something will come of it.* Nobody was around; he jumped in.

His foot landed on something hard and he rolled his ankle. As he winced in pain and cursed, he looked down and saw an empty chest. So, they *were* here last night.

He jumped out and went back into the hotel. The manager came out, and they talked for a few minutes. He said nothing was suspicious from the night before, although there were some Americans that came with a lot of luggage the night before. This was unusual because not a lot of English-speaking people came to the hotel, and he noticed them speaking it when they were at the bar having drinks. Silvio quickly thanked the manager, even though he wasn't able to provide him with any video of them. A hotel that old didn't have cameras.

Outside, Silvo lit up another cigarette. What was his next move going to be? He went back to his hotel and called Aurelio to give him the latest news. He could hear that Aurelio was extremely anxious. *What could this secret be that's so big?* he thought.

As he took a boiling hot shower and tried to figure out what to do, he thought about the wet suit in his bag. He quickly rinsed off and went to his bag and took the suit out. It was unremarkable, much like the one he had worn. There were no markings or initials on it. He was about to light up another cigarette when he realized there was an oxygen tank in his room and that would be a stupid idea. Then an idea hit him: the oxygen tank. He flipped it over and looked for the serial numbers and any special markings on it. It did have a serial number indeed and the bottom read "Made in Boston." He was able to trace the serial number to a store in Boston. That would be his next move. There he should be able to find out who had bought it.

He called Aurelio back and gave him the news. Aurelio gave him his blessing to go to Boston. It would have to wait for the morning, though. It was too late to get a flight at this time of night. He lay down in bed and planned. He knew that what he was doing was for the greater good of the Church. He just couldn't believe what he was going to be asked to do next.

Chapter Thirteen

Pope Ignatius was worried when he saw Aurelio speeding towards him. That never meant good news.

"Your Holiness, we need to talk," Aurelio said.

"What can I be of service to you with?" the Pope asked.

"We have a lead on Venice," he said.

"What would that be exactly?"

"Silvio was able to track down the empty chest in a dumpster behind a different hotel. He also found a discarded wet suit in the water. It was hanging off a log. If it hadn't gotten stuck there, we'd have nothing. Also, if we hadn't sent him yesterday when we did, the dumpster would have been cleared out and we'd literally have nothing." It sounded like Aurelio was implying that he'd made the right call. The Pope wasn't so sure yet. What if all this running around, sneaking and hiding was not what the Church was supposed to be from the beginning? He was struggling with that lately.

"What have you told him to do?" he asked.

"He's tracked down a serial number to a company in Boston. He's on his way there right now trying to get information about who purchased it," Aurelio said.

Boston? The Pope found that alarming. Could it be that he was still at it again? Thoughts raced through his mind surrounding the dizzying implication that the boy who brought down the President and exposed Jesuit activity could actually be the one on the trail of these three capstones. Somehow, he managed to keep from revealing his feelings to Aurelio.

"Collect the College of Cardinals. I need to speak with them," he instructed.

Aurelio went out to get them. He was a bit annoyed to be sent on a duty, but he was not the Pope. If only he was, he could really get things done.

After an hour or so, the cardinals gathered. The Pope was pleased they came so quickly.

"My brothers," the Pope began, "It seems that once again we're facing a great challenge within our house. It seems that the great is beginning to unravel, and we are completely blindsided by it. Someone or some people have recovered the first third of the puzzle. At this time, we don't know who, but Silvio is working on it now. We hope to have answers within a few days. What that means is that for the near future, everything must be squeaky clean. We can't afford to seem weak at a time like this."

"Excuse me, Your Holiness, but what exactly is this great secret?" Cardinal DelVecchio asked.

"None of us individually know the answer to that. It's for our own protection, so it can't be used against us," the Pope said, knowing full well that he was lying. He needed to keep this a giant secret, because the ramifications could bring this entire house to its knees. Truthfully, he knew that Aurelio didn't know either. He had just been brought up as a lifelong Jesuit knowing that this was the great secret that he was to guard with his life.

The Pope looked around and saw a lot of upset and frustrated faces. He had known that he had been losing them for a while now, while Aurelio has been growing in popularity. He had thought back to Pope John Paul I, who ruled for only 33 days. He was known as the Smiling Pope and was hated by most conservative cardinals. His death was a mystery, and Ignatius wondered for himself if one day he would share the same fate. He had also recently tried to make peace with the Jewish leaders by uncovering a scripture that was more than 1600 years old that the Vatican had rediscovered, which included the actual name of God that was revealed in the Old Testament. He had tried so hard to mend bridges, but it seemed futile at this point. Still, for now, he was in charge.

"Nobody is to act on this until further instruction from me," Pope Ignatius said.

"This is not right," Cardinal Sorrentino said.

"We already have Silvio working on this. What are you saying exactly?" a bewildered Aurelio asked.

"What I'm saying is I need some time to think about how we should approach this. It's never good to act out of fear," the Pope replied. "You are all dismissed."

One by one, people started leaving the giant hall, murmuring together. Pope Ignatius noticed Aurelio out of the corner of his eye, shaking hands with some of the cardinals and patting them on the back.

Just then the Camerlengo walked in, surprised to see everyone there. He couldn't remember a time when there were so many meetings in such a short span of time.

"Your Holiness, are you alright?" Jean-Louis asked.

"It's been a hard day," the Pope replied.

Aurelio walked into the courtyard. The Pope waited until he was long gone before he addressed his beloved Camerlengo.

"Things have not been looking good for me lately. I can feel the congregation slowly turning on me and desperately looking for someone else to lead. At times I fear for my life. At the same time, I know that what I am doing is right by God. I wish I could tell you more about what we're dealing with here, Jean-Louis, but unfortunately it would only put you at risk. I've tried very hard to keep this all a secret my entire time here at the throne, but it seems that no matter what I do, I anger those around me."

"Your Holiness, I don't know what you're into right now or what everyone has gotten themselves into, but I will always be here for you. It's my job," he said, smiling.

The Pope knew that was the truth. If there was one person he could trust and rely on, it was his Camerlengo. He so desperately wanted to tell him the greatest secret of all and what would happen if all of the treasure chests were opened. It would unleash a secret more than twice as old as Christianity itself.

Fortunately for the world and for everyone involved, when the Pope rearranged the chests throughout the world, he buried a secret in one of them. One that would be able to bring this all down in a heartbeat should he pass away and someone unlock its code. The Pope was beginning to wonder if that wasn't what he'd wanted all along.

Not far away, Aurelio was making a call in his apartment. "Hello, Silvio. I'm afraid it's time for plan B. I see no other way. No, I know you figured out where you have to go, but this takes precedence. Please come back home immediately. You will soon be able to leave again," he said, as he hung up the phone. Dark times were coming.

Chapter Fourteen

"Anybody have the slightest clue as to what this message means?" I asked. Eighty percent of what we had encountered had been anagrams. This was much more complex and full of riddles.

"I have no idea, baby," Hannah said.

"Yeah, I'm at a loss, Newsdon. This is nuts," Rosette replied.

"Well we do know the first part of it," Jackson said. "By the Hand of God discovered in the language of the people of Aries; we just saw two giant hands reaching towards the sky and Rose was able to figure out that it was a Hebrew riddle. So, we know that much."

I hadn't even thought about that, but he was right. I took a small bite of my melting Italian ice and glanced at the TV. Blur Slanders was on once again, this time talking about how soy is feminizing men with all its phytoestrogens. "Soy boys," he was calling the phenomenon. I chuckled. My mind turned to the couch where this capstone was resting.

"What are we going to do with this thing?" I asked. I didn't think anybody had a clue as to how to hide it. What if we were able to locate all three capstones? They weren't that big, but they weren't small either.

"We'll figure it out," Rosette said.

I finished my Italian ice and thought about Blur Slanders. He was the one that gave us the bump on this entire thing, and surprisingly he had been right so far. I also realized that some conspiracy theories were correct, though I hated that term. NP had hated it as well. He always used to say that the phrase "conspiracy theory" was started by the CIA in response to people who didn't accept the narrative of the Kennedy Assassination. It's a lowbrow attack on someone to call them that.

"Do you guys know why God is a man and Earth is a woman?" Rosette asked.

We all shot her quizzical looks.

"It's because God's shemen, which incidentally is Hebrew for oil, which is why early Christians were baptized in oil, Christ also meaning oil, would come down throughout the year but more specifically during Taurus. It's also where we get the word semen from. You've heard of the saying 'April showers bring May flowers'? You plant the seeds during Taurus, you put the plow on the bull or Taurus and plow the land. Then God's shemen would impregnate Mother Earth, and life would grow from her. This would culminate in August and September. In August Virgo, the virgin with the wheat stalk, would be when the virgins would go out into the field and cultivate the wheat so you could make the bread.

September is when you would cultivate the grapes and make the wine. The bread and the wine, the two symbols of Christianity. This is how God's Sun would have the ability to turn water into wine. Also, the Jewish holiday Shavuot used to be a wheat harvest holiday which sur- prise surprise, falls during Taurus," she finished.

Who the fuck was this girl channeling, her inner NP?

"Where did that all come from, girl?" I asked.

"I dated a super Jewish kid, remember? Also, I have been thinking about NP a lot lately and just followed the trail of thought that he mentioned to me before," Her voice trailed off. We were all still pretty raw from his loss.

"It really does make sense, if you think about it," I said. "Regarding the wheat, there's a phrase in the Bible that goes, 'Those too lazy to plow in the right season will have no food at the harvest.' I believe it's Proverbs 20:4. People use that phrase to talk about planning for im- portant things in their life, but it literally could just mean that you need to plant in Taurus, or you won't get shit a few months later."

"Call me crazy, but at the end of John, Jesus says, 'It is finished.' Many people take that to mean his work is done, but right before he dies, he's given a sip of vinegar. Vinegar is nothing but wine past its prime. He could have literally just been talking about the wine, saying that it is finished aging," I said.

"Wait, I have an idea. This has always seemed to be a running theme in each thing we've had to figure out. What if we keep applying that logic to this puzzle?" Hannah asked.

"Go on," I said.

"Well, just take a look at this. As Jax mentioned, we know the first part so far. Let's break it down piece by piece. They're saying that the second stone should have to do with Pisces. Right after that it says the ruling planet stood vigilant. What's the ruling planet of Pisces?"

"I'm pretty sure it's Jupiter. No wait, Neptune," I added.

"So, Neptune stood vigilant and kept watch over it, it can only mean the location, until it was brought down in the last days of the rooster. What does that mean?" she asked.

"There's no rooster in the zodiac," Jackson said.

"But there is in the Chinese one," I said.

"At the hands of the Scorpion, so we know that's Scorpio, I see where you're going with this, Husker. By the way, when are you two getting married?" Rose asked.

"What goes on in your brain that makes you think this is a good time to discuss this?" I asked. "Is there anything else up there that you'd like to ask?"

"I was just wondering why Aunt Jemima and Uncle Ben never got together to create rice pancakes," she said.

"Can I buy some weed from you?" I asked.

"Shut up, you two mental midgets," Hannah said. "Where were we?"

"Towards the last days of the Fish," Jackson said.

"Thank you, Jax," Hannah said. "We know that's Pisces, so the question is, what happened during the last days of that Chinese Year, in Scorpio preferably, towards the end of Pisces?" Hannah asked.

We sat there for a few minutes staring at each other. What did Neptune have to do with it? I understood that the clues referenced three animals, but this was just the wedge in between it all.

"Did you know that Leonardo DaVinci's last supper was a coded reference to the Zodiac?" I asked.

"How now?" Hannah said.

"I don't really know all of them, but one of the signs point to Mary Magdalene, more specifically her Adam's Apple, or lack thereof. The apostle holding up both hands signifies the Twins in Gemini. The man in the green spreading his arms signifies the scales of justice in Libra. Things of that nature," I said.

"That's really cool and all, but we need to figure this shit out," Rosette said.

We continued thinking about it, and we started getting anxious, realizing that we had to get this right. God knows what we had started by finding the first one. I kept thinking about a quote I read once: 'the most brilliant logic based upon a wrong assumption produces an elegantly formulated incorrect result.'

"Wait, guys," Jackson said. "What if the animals are meant to be taken as signs of the right time, but Neptune was meant to be taken literally?" he asked.

"What do you mean by that?" I said.

"The Year of the Rooster isn't until 2029. It was last in 2005. This was nearing the last days of Pisces, the fish. The last days were Scorpio in 2005."

"Seriously awesome, bro," I said. "But what about Neptune?"

"There's a fountain of Neptune in Florence," Rosette interjected.

"Shit, we have to go back to Italy again?" Hannah winced.

"Not so fast," Jackson said. "There's a statue in Virginia Beach as well."

"This isn't help . . . oh my God, wait!" Rosette shrieked. "The last Hand to God we saw was a literal Hand to God. I know that sounds stupid, whatever, you know what I mean. But we're looking for another Hand to God. That's how these are to be located. We just have to find the giant sculptures," she smiled. "Like this for instance." She turned her laptop on to show us.

"This is a statue of Neptune, in the Canary Islands in an area called Gran Canaria. And look at what else I found." She was smiling ear to ear. I love when she gets like this. "This is a famous rock called 'El Dedo De Dios.' Or literally, the Finger of God. I was reading up on it and in November of 2005 a tropical storm came in and knocked the finger off. This has to be it. Neptune still watching over it."

"This is unbelievable, Rose. You've definitely nailed it." My excitement soured, though, when I realized I was going to have to fucking dive again.

"When are we leaving?" Hannah asked.

"I'm already looking up flights," Rosette said.

"Guys, I'm going to have to sit this one out," Jackson said.

"Why, baby?" Rose asked.

"I just can't make this trip right now. I need to go visit my family for my birthday. You know I do that every year, right?"

"Are you sure? We really could use you," I pleaded.

"Sorry, bud. But in the meantime, I'll figure out where to hide this monstrosity. Give me a call when you get back into town," he said.

As he left our house, we sat back, sad but understanding. Rose and Hannah finished up our travel arrangements while I made myself some tea. I know, I lead such a rock star lifestyle.

All so-called revealed religions consist mainly of three portions. A cosmogony more or less mythical, a history more or less falsified and a moral code more or less pure. - Richard Burton

Chapter Fifteen

We boarded the plane to Barcelona. We didn't want to make a scene, so we booked the first row in coach. We settled in and I flipped open my phone to check my emails. I had one message from Blur Slanders. He was hoping everything was going well with our travels and left me a link to *loveforlife.au* to check out. Something he had been talking about that day.

I opened it up and started reading about a man named Frank O'Collins in Australia who was becoming an underground king against the globalists. Was that all he thought about? This Frank was apparently writing about how Canon Law can be used in the courts to manipulate the system and get any charge against you thrown out. He claimed to have examples of people who, by saying the right things, could get the judge to bow and recuse himself from the case. Apparently, your birth certificate establishes you as a fictitious entity. The way they trick you into it is that they have your name all in capital letters, which is not your given name. The judge tries to get you to admit to this 'character' in court when he asks your name. The key is to give your first name only or nickname. Until you admit that you are that character, no charges can be brought against you.

He was also saying that judges wear black because it can be traced back to the worship of the planet Saturn or the black planet. That made sense to me, as I had read recently that Saturn worship dates back many millennia. The Jews wear the black box on their head and the Muslims walk around a giant black box in Mecca called the Kaaba. Even the Catholic clergy wear something called the cappello romano, which is a hat with a ring reminiscent of the ringed planet Saturn. It's also why the Jews have their day of rest on the Saturn day or Saturday. It's also why women get their ears pierced and wear earrings. Men used to tell them they had to listen to their God (Saturn), so they would wear rings to honor him. Wedding rings as well.

Anyway, the birth certificate is publicly traded on the stock market. It enrolls you into the "system" and your future labor is used as collateral for generating debt. O'Collins went into how everything is about maritime law. For example, when you pull a boat into the "dock" or "berth," the first thing you have to do is produce a certificate of manifest. When you're having a child or giving "birth" the "doc" is the one who delivers the baby and the certificate of "birth" is the certificate of manifest. It's also why when you're sending packages by land or air it's called "shipping." Really cool stuff, actually. But unfortunately, Rosette interrupted my reading. I had been keeping tabs on her. She was already two drinks deep, since she hated flying.

"We are the epitome of the arousal theory," she said.

"What's that now?" I asked.

"This crazy trip that we've been on for almost a year. Never in my life would I have thought that we'd be going through so much," she said.

"Very true, girl. How are you feeling?" Hannah asked.

"I'm fine. I took a Xanny before we boarded the plane. The question is how are you two sexy bitches doing?"

"What?" I said.

"You two are such a sexy looking couple. Tell me. Do you swing?" she asked.

"Ha ha, what?" Hannah replied. I was too surprised to answer.

"I'm sorry, that was rude of me. Here, Newsdon, let me ask you a question. A psychological question, so please answer honestly," she said.

"I'll try my best," I said.

"Have you ever given Husker the Woodcock Johnson test before?" she asked, smiling.

"Rosette, stop it." Hannah couldn't control her laughter. Xanax and alcohol was a serious mental muscle relaxer for this girl.

"I'm sorry. I can't help myself. It's going down, I'm yelling Tinder," she sang.

"Did you just say Tinder, don't you mean timber?" I asked.

"I know what I said, thank you."

Thankfully, this only lasted another twenty minutes and then she was out like a light, and we were all able to get some rest.

We landed in Barcelona and had a two-hour layover until our flight to Gran Canaria. The Canary Islands are basically Spain's Hawaii. We sat at the food court until it was time to board. The flight was short and uneventful; Rosette slept again, and Hannah was playing a word scramble game on her phone.

We landed in Gran Canaria, got our luggage and walked out the door. The heat was blistering. We rented a car and made the short drive to Puerto de los Nievas and checked into the Casa Del Mar hotel. We unpacked, and I worked on getting into my new wet suit. This time, though, besides the oxygen tank and the mask, I also got an X2 sports underwater jetpack. The canal was one thing, but this was the ocean. There were waves and I wasn't about to get caught in an underwater riptide.

I realized I couldn't suit up and walk around dressed like a crazy person, so I just stayed in my wet suit and put the rest in a duffel bag. We went back out to the car and drove down the road until the rock was in sight. We barely noticed it without the giant finger still standing up on it, but there it was. It was a steep cliff to get down, so I was going to have to swim farther than I had before. I took out my phone and snapped a picture for comparison.

It was a good thing I had bought a larger oxygen tank than the previous one that had almost run out on me.

"Wish me luck, girls," I said.

"You'll be fine, Newsdon," Rosette said.

"No, this is not fine, actually. I'm never going to make it. There has to be a better way," I said. Luckily, there was a place nearby that rented boats. We picked one up, and we left the car by the side of the road near the water.

We got into the boat and headed towards the rock monument. We were about fifty feet away when I suited up and fell backward into the water.

It was some of the warmest water I'd ever been in. I popped my head out of the water to judge direction and then went back under. I felt something swim by me and my body froze in fear. Then I remembered that vending machines kill four times as many people as sharks every year, and I calmed right down. I was actually swimming with the tide, almost.

When I got to the stone, I looked up to see if anyone could see me. I was secluded down there, so I searched the stone. Nothing on top. Okay, then. I went underwater and started circling the thing. Nothing for about fifteen feet. I started to get nervous. I was turning the corner when my foot got stuck in a wedge. I looked down and there it was. The second chest, staring at me.

I pulled it out and surfaced. I waved at the girls and they sped toward me, hiding on the backside of the stone in case anybody was looking. They helped lift the chest out of the water onto the boat and put a blanket over it while I slumped, out of breath.

We sped back to where the car was parked and loaded the chest into the trunk. Rosette then jumped back into the boat and returned it. Hannah and I picked her up about a quarter mile away.

"So, what do you think this one is, baby?" Hannah asked.

"I have no idea. I didn't even get to look at it. I'm almost too nervous to see what's on it or how it opens," I said.

Rosette jumped in the car and we sped back to the hotel, stopping to pick up takeout along the way. We sneaked the chest into our room, and I yanked the blanket off like I was ripping a bandage off a wound.

It was much more sophisticated than the one we had previously encountered. This was some kind of metal that didn't seem to rust. Of course, there was a 4 digit pass code again. It had a saying etched onto it and a picture engraved under it.

Life in Life while Death surrounds. It's the maker's Mark.

"Not this life, two times life shit again," Rosette said.

"I'm lost," Hannah said.

"Yeah, I'm going to go with a no on this one," Rosette said.

We ate dinner while looking at the thing. Something about it was familiar, I just couldn't quite put my finger on it. Not the numbers, but the design. I knew it from somewhere. Was it the Olympics? No, not quite. Finally, it came to me. It was called the Egg of Life.

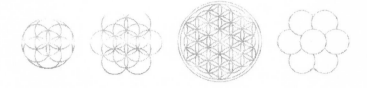

I had read about it in a book called the *Flower of Life* by Drunvalo Melchizadek, all about sacred geometry. It had inspired the Spirit Science series on AquaStream.

In the book, he mentioned that the Egg of Life was how the first cells divided during gestation. Looking it up on my phone, I could see that to be true. So that must be one life. But what about the other? What were these numbers all about? We tried to figure out if there were any patterns in them, but we couldn't. We decided to call it a night and go to sleep. I had my own bed and Rosette and Hannah shared the other one so that things weren't too third-wheelish.

We couldn't believe that we'd been holed up in a hotel for two days trying to figure this shit out. It was blowing our minds. Rosette more mentioned than a few times that NP would have been a great help; even Jackson might have used his physics magic on the box. Finally, at the point of madness, we had a breakthrough.

"Goddammit box, why have you forsaken me?" Rosette said.

"Isn't that Biblical?" Hannah replied. She had not gone to Catholic school or been given a Confirmation Bible.

"Sure is. So nice, he said it twice," Rosette laughed.

"That's terrible. Also, he only said it once," I replied.

"Try again, choir boy," Rosette shot back.

"No, I'm pretty sure he said it once. He said something different in all four gospels," I countered.

"Look it up. There's probably a Gideon Bible in that drawer right there," she said.

"Fuck it, I need a break anyway," I said.

I turned to the little table that the lamp was sitting on. Sure enough, there was a Bible in the drawer. I opened it to a random page. Luke 22:10. "Behold, when you have entered the city, a man will meet you carrying a pitcher of water." Well that was just Aquarius, but not what I was looking for. I flipped to the Book of Matthew and found it. OK, so he did say it once. I went to the end of Mark and sure enough, it was there. I slammed the book shut. I looked at the box and a lightning bolt of memory came through. I opened Matthew again. The verse where Jesus asked why he was being forsaken was Matthew 27:46.

"Hey guys, take a look at this," I said.

I explained to them what I had found and based on that, Rosette said that the 3:16 in the middle must be John 3:16, the most famous Bible verse of all time. "For God so loved the world that he gave his one and only Son, that whoever believes in him shall not perish but have eternal life." Yes, life. This was the life, within the Egg of Life. While death surrounds. I opened up to Mark and went to the end where Jesus dies, and it was 15:34. I looked back at the box and this wasn't on it. I slumped back down disappointed—back to square one again.

"Shit guys, I thought we had a good thing going here," I said.

"Did you check the other two death verses?" Rosette asked. "Luke and John, you tool," she said.

Expecting nothing, I opened up. Luke 23:46 was where Jesus says, "Into your hands I commend my spirit." Luke 19:30 was where he said, "It is finished." Well, whatever he really meant by that. The missing one was Mark. The "Maker's Mark." God's gospel of Mark. Of course!

I punched 1534 into the keypad and it opened up. There it was: another capstone. Same size as the first one. There was also a small vial of liquid with a message written in Italian scribbled on it. I couldn't really tell what it was, it looked like some thin gelatinous liquid in the middle of some kind of media. That didn't matter. We had to get home.

We packed up our things and headed back to the airport. Our flight wasn't for a few hours, but we checked in and sat down to enjoy a drink. It's amazing what you can get away with when you put a pricing sticker on a capstone. It's not like anybody in the normal world knows what they even look like or what they are.

Rose tried to call Jackson. He didn't pick up. That was odd and not like him. I started feeling Cherophobic. Every time I start to feel happy, I stop myself because bad things are around the corner. Some call that pessimistic or as I call it, old school Italian. Rosette and Jackson always talked around this time, unless they were together.

Chapter Sixteen

The Camerlengo walked slowly down the hallway to visit Pope Ignatius. This entire ordeal had become a little much for him, and he was looking for spiritual guidance. If there was one thing Ignatius could provide, it was that. He had always considered him more of a friend than His Holiness. He turned a corner to walk down another long corridor. There were so many twists and turns, he didn't know where to begin half the time. He finally made it to the room and knocked on the door. He had planned on just peppering him with questions about what had gone missing and if there was any way that he would be able to help. Truth was, the Pope had always thought of him as much of a friend as well.

"Come in," a voice on the inside said.

That was odd. The Pope never usually has guests at this time. He opened the door to the last thing he ever imagined he could see.

There was Aurelio standing over the pope with the silver hammer. The Camerlengo's confusion turned into horror when he realized what that meant.

"Good, you're just in time," Aurelio said.

"What happened?" Jean-Louis asked.

"Hold on a minute," Aurelio said.

He then proceeded to tap the Pope's forehead three times very slowly, calling him by his Christian name each time. The Pope sat there, eyes closed and motionless. This was just the beginning of the Camerlengo's nightmare.

"That's my job, and we don't actually do that anymore," Jean-Louis said.

"I'm a bit old school, you could say," Aurelio said. "Alas, I'm afraid that Pope Ignatius I has passed away."

The Camerlengo felt a sick feeling in the pit of his stomach. He didn't understand. The Pope was just fine hours earlier. Also, how was Aurelio the first person to find him? And how did he get that hammer? He must have snuck into his office. Something about this was not adding up at all.

"Camerlengo, I have to let you know that we're in the middle of a crisis right now, so things are going to go a little bit differently around here. We're not waiting fifteen days, we're holding conclave tonight. I'm going to need you to round up the cardinals as soon as possible. Thank you," Aurelio said.

"But that's not how things work. You don't get to declare conclave," a very confused Jean-Louis said.

"Things come in and out of our structure all the time. As you so humbly pointed out, we don't use the hammer anymore. Things change sometimes. Now please do it," Aurelio said.

The Camerlengo shut the door behind him and began walking slowly towards the Sistine Chapel where mass was being held. It was also the place where they would hole up for conclave. No one else was aware of what had just taken place. If only there was somebody he could talk to about all of this.

The Camerlengo climbed the stairs and went inside. He waited until the mass had ended before he addressed everyone. They were all shocked to see him and even more so that he was speaking to them there.

"I don't know where to begin right now. Pope Ignatius I has passed away," he said.

There were gasps in the crowd, which slowly turned into murmurs. Murmurs became loud talking.

"How do we know this?" Cardinal DelVecchio asked.

"I was just in his common area with Aurelio. I saw him with my own eyes," he said.

More murmurs.

"And he didn't respond to his name? Why was Aurelio there?" Asked Cardinal Sorrentino.

"I have no idea when he got there, but he did not respond to his name or the hammer," he said.

"The hammer has been discontinued. Why did you use the hammer, Camerlengo?" Cardinal DelVecchio asked.

"I did not use the hammer. Aurelio did. He insisted on it. He asked me to come here and collect you all. He calls for conclave tonight due to emergency," Jean-Louis said.

Loud murmurs erupted.

"Who is he to call for conclave?" Cardinal DelVecchio asked angrily.

"I'm just repeating a message. Do with it what you like," he said.

He walked slowly back to his office. He felt a lump in his throat form, and he became short of breath. He stopped for a minute, hands on knees, hunched over as he tried to regain composure. He decided he had to sit down on the bench to catch himself.

He sat and tried to calm down. It wasn't working. It didn't help that he lived with an anxiety disorder to begin with. His pills were in his office. This was definitely one of those Seroquel moments. He stood up and with shaking knees, started to walk away when he was called.

"Camerlengo, come back," Cardinal DelVecchio said.

He turned around and took a deep breath.

"We've discussed it, and we are going to hold conclave tonight," the cardinal said.

"What do you need from me?" Jean-Louis said.

"Bolt the door."

The Camerlengo followed Cardinal DelVecchio back to the Sistine Chapel, and once he was inside, he locked the door. He couldn't fathom what was happening right now. They hadn't even buried Ignatius. They hadn't alerted the media. He was beside himself. Once the door was locked, he turned and ran back to his office and popped one of his pills. He sat down and twenty minutes later he felt like he had drunk twelve beers. He passed out in the chair. He only woke up four hours later when Cardinal Sorrentino entered the room.

"Camerlengo, wake up. It's done," he said.

The Camerlengo, still groggy, rubbed his eyes and looked up. Then the anxiety hit him again like a ton of bricks. He looked outside and there was white smoke billowing from the chimney. He looked at the clock. A new Pope in four hours? This can't be. He must have slept for days. He looked at his watch and he was wrong. It had been four hours. Has it ever been this fast before? Is this even possible?

"Who has been selected?" he asked the Cardinal.

"Pope Aurora Toss I," Cardinal Sorrentino said.

"Who? What?" he replied.

"You remember him as Aurelio," Cardinal Sorrentino said, absorbing the bewildered look on the Camerlengo's face before he turned to the door and left.

The Camerlengo couldn't believe what had just happened. Six hours ago he was going to talk to an old friend about an issue they were having, and now he was going to crown a new Pope. His anxiety wasn't helping either. But it did remind him why he seldom took those pills. They took the anxiety away, but they left him like an infant. He stood up and walked out the door towards his living quarters, thinking that if he could just get a good night's sleep, he would be able to figure things out in the morning. As he reached his door and turned the knob, he heard a familiar voice behind him.

"Hello, Camerlengo," Aurelio said.

"Hello, Aurelio," he replied. He couldn't believe he was going to have to refer to him as His Holiness. This was not OK with him. Something about all of this didn't add up.

"You know, I've been dreaming about wearing the responsibility of the Ring of the Fisherman my entire life. Since you are so by the book," he trailed off and handed Jean-Louis the ring.

The Camerlengo's stomach turned again. He felt like he was going to dry heave. It was his job to put the Ring of the Fisherman on the new Pope's hand, which he did begrudgingly.

"Here you go, Aurelio," he said.

Aurelio smiled at the Camerlengo for a moment and then took a step forward.

"Camerlengo," the Pope began, "Firstly, you will address me as Your Holiness. Hell, you can even address me as Aurora. You know that I used to love horses, but this is the only Triple Crown I care about now. Now, it isn't unlikely for the new Pope to replace the Camerlengo. So, what I need to know is the following," he said, as he took another step forward. They were about a foot apart now. "If I ask you to hold the umbraculum for me, would you?" he smirked.

"We don't do that anymore, either," the Camerlengo replied, regretting it instantly.

Still smirking, the Pope said, "Please don't make me ask you again."

Camerlengo considered his options. He turned and saw Silvio walking towards them. He looked the Pope square in the eye and said, "I would, Your Holiness."

Aurelio looked at the Camerlengo and his smirk slowly turned into a big smile. "Well, that's very good to know. Ah, Silvio. So great to see you my friend, where have you been?" he said.

"I've been waiting for your instructions, Your Holiness," he replied.

"Ah, good, good. Well, I believe everything is in order right now—most of it, that is. Your work here is done. You're free to go to Boston. Please bring us back some good news," the Pope said.

"I'm already packed. My flight leaves in two hours," Silvio said.

"What flight leaves this late at night going against the time zones?" Camerlengo asked.

Pope Aurora smiled at him with that big creepy smile again. "'The Shepherd One' of course. Now gentlemen, you'll have to excuse me, I've got plenty of work to do."

Both the Pope and Silvio left the Camerlengo alone with his thoughts. He took a deep breath. What did the Pope mean, 'your work is done'? He still couldn't get over how fast this had all occurred. Something was definitely up. He returned to his apartment and crawled into bed. He was going to sleep and wash this nightmare off of him. Well, first he took his Melatonin. He used to take Lunesta, until the nightmares started to hit him. Poor Ignatius. He did not deserve to be under St. Peter's Basilica yet. As he dozed off, his last thought was that he was going to go to Silvio's apartment to look for clues. The other man was going to be in Boston; he would just have to wait for the nighttime so nobody saw him.

Chapter Seventeen

The Camerlengo woke up refreshed. He always enjoyed that thirty seconds of peace in the morning when he woke up, before his brain kicked in and reminded him about the day before. He showered and made his coffee and went to work.

The press was in full cry, as many people had seen the white smoke the night before and a huge crowd had gathered in St. Peter's Square. A riot almost broke out, as it was the first time ever that a new Pope had announced before news of the old Pope's passing had spread. They were calling it a heart attack. But who the hell knew. Popes were not autopsied.

After dealing with the press all morning and afternoon, Jean-Louis put his coat on and left the office. He went home and took a Xanax. Just enough to take the edge off but not enough to make him loopy. He sat and planned his night out.

A few hours later at dusk, the Camerlengo left his apartment and walked the half mile to Silvio's apartment. At the door, he looked around to see if anybody was there. He pulled the lock pick set out of his pocket. It had been eons since he had last done this, but now was as good a time as ever to see if he still had it. After fidgeting with the bottom lock, he tried to open the door. It was still locked. He attempted to pick the second lock and open the door. Still locked. Frustrated, he walked around the side of the apartment to look in the window at the locks. There were four of them, but he saw that he had actually locked one of them. Interesting. Silvio had four locks, but he only locked two of them, that way if someone tried to break in, they would always lock two. The Camerlengo walked back to the door and unlocked the appropriate locks.

He entered the apartment and quickly shut the door behind him. It was dark. He pulled out a flashlight from his pocket and started looking around. He scanned everything from floor to ceiling and was unable to find anything. Frustrated and about to leave, he felt a spider fall on his hand. He jumped and stepped on it out of habit. *Shit*, he thought. Silvio would notice that on the floor in a heartbeat.

He went into the kitchen to get a paper towel and cleaned up the spider. He opened the cabinet under the kitchen sink to throw it out and noticed something that seemed out of place. There was a Ziploc baggie of white powder there. He thought it could have been cocaine at first, but then he noticed there were beans in the bag. He reached into a cabinet above the sink and grabbed another plastic bag. He took some of the powder and a few beans and tucked it away into his jacket. He shut the cabinet and exited the house, careful to relock the appropriate locks.

The Camerlengo returned to his apartment, heart pounding. He took another Xanax and waited for forty-five minutes until it kicked in. Those forty-five minutes were hell on earth. He wished that God would just release him from this crippling invisible disease that he carried. Eventually he felt a little bit better and was able to function.

He opened the baggie and took out the beans and placed them on the table. He looked at the powder. He put it close to his face and smelled it. Odorless. He licked his fingertip and dipped it in the bag and tasted it. Tasteless. Definitely not cocaine. Tired, he left the beans and powder on the table and went to bed. He took a melatonin capsule, but as he was about to fall asleep, he felt a sharp pain in his stomach and could not catch his breath. There was anxiety, too, but this was completely different. He felt like his insides were being ripped apart. He ran to the bathroom and threw up for an hour, until he was so exhausted that he just passed out next to the toilet.

He woke up in the morning drained and dehydrated. He tried to remember what he had eaten the night before that had caused him such pain. He was slightly lactose intolerant but had never had these symptoms.

He opened his laptop and looked up his symptoms on the internet. Sweating, tightness in the chest, nausea and vomiting. It could have been any number of things. He scrolled until something made him stop, and start sweating all over again.

He picked up one of the beans from the table, returned to the computer and looked up castor beans. They were an identical match. The Camerlengo popped another Xanax and sat back in his chair. Last night he had accidentally ingested a bit of pure ricin. Was this what had happened to his friend Pope Ignatius? Had he been poisoned?

Chapter Eighteen

Silvio landed in Boston after a very turbulent flight. He was a bit nauseous when he got off the plane. He bought some Pepto-Bismol and Alka-Seltzer in the airport. *This is what happens when you start to get old*, he thought to himself.

He was only forty, but he was a dinosaur compared to the Swiss Guard. He was still a legend there. The Pope had been making a local visit and someone had come at him with a gun. With only seconds to react, he raised his halberd and took the guy's left eye out of his head. It had been the closest anybody had come to assassinating the Pope since John Paul II. He still laughed about it to this day. He took those days seriously. The second he got out of the guard, he got a huge *Acriter et Fideliter* tattoo across his chest.

He left the airport in a rental car. He used the GPS on his phone instead of the one in the car. He didn't want anyone to trace his steps, should something come of this. He drove directly to the dive store and parked around the corner. He didn't want them to see his car.

He got out of the car and tucked his gun into his pants and pulled his shirt over it. He was able to get through customs with his gun by flashing his Swiss Guard badge.

It didn't matter that it had been expired for years, his thumb covered the date when he flashed it. He walked around the corner and into the store. There was one other person in the store with him and the clerk. He weighed his options.

"Hello, how can I help you?" the store clerk asked.

"Hello. My name is Steve and my brother was here a few days ago purchasing an oxygen tank. I would like to see the receipt," he said.

"Do you have any ID?" the clerk asked.

Silvio hesitated. He did not want to give him his ID in case this went sour. "I don't, I'm sorry but I can tell you the date and time that it was purchased. He bought it with his credit card," Silvio said.

"I'm sorry, but without ID or you telling me what this is about, I cannot help you," the clerk said and turned to go to the back.

Silvio stood there trying to figure out his next move. He looked outside to see if there were any police. There weren't. He sat in a chair in the corner and waited for the other customer to leave, which he finally did. He stood up and went to the counter and rang the bell.

"Hello again," Silvio said with a smile.

"Look, without ID I cannot help you. I'm going to have to ask you to leave," the store clerk demanded.

Silvio always hated this part. It gave him a rush of adrenaline, but he always hoped to solve problems without violence. He grabbed the clerk's head and slammed it on the counter. Dizzy and in pain, the clerk backed up and fell to the ground. Silvio turned the 'Open' sign on the door to 'Closed' and walked back to the clerk, who was trying to pick himself up off the ground. Silvio looked him in the eye and lifted his shirt to show his gun. The clerk's eyes grew as wide as oranges as he stood up.

"Let's try this again," Silvio said. "Believe me, I have no desire to hurt you, but I must have that ticket."

"OK, OK. Just please don't hit me again," the store clerk said.

He flipped through the receipts until he came to Jackson's name. "Here. This is him. He came to the store in a huge rush. Please don't hurt me," he said.

"I'm not going to hurt you. But if I were you, I wouldn't call the police about this. This is an international investigation," Silvio said as he unlocked the door and disappeared around the corner.

Silvio got into his car and took off as the police were arriving. He didn't even hold it against the clerk for calling the police. This had probably shaken his world, and he would have nightmares over it.

Silvio parked a few blocks away and changed into a jumpsuit, putting his suit in the trunk. He put on a hat and sunglasses and took a look at the receipt. He had Jackson's full address.

The fifty-minute trip was uneventful. Silvio didn't even get butterflies anymore when he was getting himself into something like this. Chalk it up to experience. He pulled up to Jackson and Rosette's address in Chestnut Hill. This was the home of Boston College, one of the premier Jesuit education centers in the world, he reminded himself. He parked his car a block away and came back to the door. They had a townhouse, so he had to be very quick in getting in; the nearest neighbor was just ten feet away. He took out his lock pick and quickly opened the door.

There was nobody home. This disappointed Silvio. He was a big fan of things going smoothly. He went in the bathroom to pee and looked around. There were pictures of Jackson and his girlfriend everywhere. He took note of Jackson's size and build. He had never had a problem dealing with someone like that, but he was getting a bit older. He shook his nerves away and went upstairs to see if he could find anything, careful not to move anything or leave fingerprints. Silvio always carried a pair of gloves with him.

It occurred to him to sit down and wait for Jackson to return. This was the man who was responsible for all the drama in the Vatican and Silvio felt a rage build up in him. He didn't know what was in these treasure chests or what their purpose was, but he was fully committed to the Vatican and especially to Aurelio. It has literally been his life's work and purpose.

He sat down in the living room and began sharpening his knife. He did that when he was bored. He looked around the living room and saw something that sent him into a blind rage. There was a picture of Jackson and his girlfriend with that kid who had taken down the President and made things so complicated for the Church.

It had never occurred to him that Jackson might be working with someone. It certainly never occurred to him that that kid Graham was involved in this as well. What was it about this kid that made him want to get involved with everything? It was then that Silvio realized he wasn't after Jackson, he was after Graham.

He stood up to leave. He knew that the Pope would be busy, so he called up the Camerlengo. He told him who he was looking for and what he had found out. He also told him that he was going to Graham's house to end this problem before it became bigger than it should be. He hung up and made another brief phone call to one of his contacts. After a moment, he received a text message from his contact with Graham's address. He left the house, returned to his car, took a deep breath and started the forty-minute drive to Quincy.

It was an uneventful car ride. He pulled up and got out of the car, walked down the driveway and opened the front door quietly. He was going to make Graham rue the day he ever screwed with the Church. He closed the door quietly and locked it behind him.

Chapter Nineteen

We finally touched down at Logan International Airport. We got our car from long term parking and Hannah drove towards Rosette's house. We were planning on recuperating for a day before we connected again to figure out what exactly we were dealing with.

The ride was uneventful. I slept while they talked and listened to the new Rising CD. We pulled up to Rosette's place and said our goodbyes. We got about two blocks away before she called us back to the house.

"What's up, girl?" Hannah said.

"He's not here," Rosette said. "I'm beginning to get worried. I haven't heard from him in a little while and that's very unlike him."

She ended up getting back in the car with us and came to our house. We figured she would just calm down and spend some time with us until we heard from Jackson.

We pulled up and parked in the back parking lot. We got all of our stuff out of the car and entered the house. I heard Rosette scream and dropped everything and ran to the living room. What I saw would haunt me for a long time.

The chairs were turned over, the table in the middle of the room was broken and there was glass everywhere. A man we'd never seen before lay dead in one corner of the room. In the opposite corner of the room sat Jackson, breathing heavily with a gash on his arm and a slice in his stomach. Rosette shook him.

"Baby, baby! Wake up. What happened here?" she squealed.

"Huh, what's going on?" he asked, disoriented.

Hannah came in the room, saw everything, and screamed.

I went over to the dead man. I put my fingers on his neck to feel for a pulse; nothing. He had a black eye and a knife sticking out of his abdomen, and a basketball-sized bruise surrounding the knife wound. I stuck my hand in his pocket and pulled out his wallet. I went through it and found an ID card from the Swiss Guard. Who the fuck was Silvio Bruno?

I'd been waiting for this moment, I just never thought it would happen like this. *The Vatican is sending people after us now for what we are doing, for what we have done in the past.* I shuddered to think that this could have been me had I not been away. I took one look at the knife and knew what had happened.

Jackson had been in the house, probably watching TV, when this man came in and crept upstairs. There was a struggle. Jackson got cut twice but was able to over-power him and stabbed him with the knife. Based on his bruise, I knew this wasn't a normal knife. My brother had told me about the latest technology, a special type of knife Special Forces carried. It was called a WASP Injector Knife. When you stab someone with it, there is a button you can press that shoots out 850 psi of carbon dioxide into the body. This freezes the internal organs. If Silvio didn't die from the initial stabbing, organ failure would have done the trick.

I sat down in a chair. This was hitting me rather hard. This should have been me, not Jackson. I thought about NP and my brother and was suddenly overwhelmed with anxiety.

"Newsdon, come over here," Rosette said.

I had a short conversation with Jackson. He was in and out. I tried to keep him awake.

"How do you feel, bro?" I asked.

"Ever hear of Schrödingers cat?" he asked.

"What?"

"It's a physics thing. So basically, there's a cat in a box with a radioactive isotope. If it smacks it, it will kill it. If it leaves it alone, it won't. In physics, the observation of something collapses the wave function. But until it's observed, it remains in both super positions. So, until you open the box to see if it's alive or dead, it's actually both alive and dead."

"That doesn't make any sense to me," I replied.

"Well it might not, but that's how I feel right now. I feel like I'm alive and dead." Even in his current state, he still had time to make a physics related joke. God, did I sound this nerdy when I was still in med school?

"We have to call an ambulance!" Rosette shrieked.

"Not yet. We have to call the police first. Don't touch anything," I said.

We decided that the right thing to do would be to call Officer Hitchlords. We called his precinct and asked for him and told him to come down right away.

After about thirty minutes, he showed up with a few other officers. They came in, looked around and did their police work.

"How are you feeling, buddy? Can you tell me what happened?" Hitchlords asked Jackson.

Just as I expected, Jackson told him he was in the living room watching TV and doing pushups when he heard the door open and close. He knew that we were overseas, so he hid behind the wall until he saw this man Silvio come into the room.

Jackson saw the knife on his bootstrap and jumped him before he could be jumped himself. There was a struggle and Jackson slipped and fell on the floor. Had he not slipped at that moment, the knife would have gone through his stomach instead of just grazing him. There was some more struggle, and Jackson was finally able to overpower him. He asked him who he was and what he wanted, but Silvio only told him that his friends had made a big mistake messing with the Church and that this was not the end. Jackson then took the knife and stabbed him with it and pressed the button on the outside of the knife. He had never seen a knife like that before, usually the military carry knives with a blood channel in them. It's an indention in the blade so that you can't stop the bleeding.

"I'm not sure what he meant about the Church, but this looks consistent with what we're seeing here. Have any of you touched anything here since you got here?" he asked us.

"No, officer," I said.

"Graham, I honestly have no idea why I keep having to see your face around crime scenes. I don't know what you get yourself into, but if it were up to me, I'd tell you to knock it out. You only have nine lives, kid," Hitchlords said, and walked over to talk to the other officers.

"Shit, baby, where is the first capstone?" Rosette asked, tears in her eyes.

"I went to Jean's vault and put it in there. I didn't think it was safe in our homes," Jackson said.

"OK, everyone. The ambulance is on its way here. Nobody go anywhere until we get him into it," Hitchlords said.

After about twenty more minutes, the ambulance came, and Jackson was loaded into it. Rosette came up to us before she got in the ambulance to go with him.

"I just wanted to say that I love you guys," she began. "But when it comes to men in my life, it's the fucking hedgehog's dilemma." She started crying as she entered the ambulance.

That just broke my heart. The Hedgehog's Dilemma is a psychological term regarding human intimacy. It wants to snuggle against another animal but can't be-cause of its needles stabbing them. It basically says that humans with good intentions can't be intimate without harming one another. I wanted to tell her that Jackson was not her fault. I knew she was referring to NP as well. I wanted to tell her that what happened to NP was not her fault. The poor girl thought that everyone she got inti-mate with got hurt.

"Alright. We've taken statements and this looks like a clear-cut case of self-defense. We'll be out of here with the body in twenty minutes," Hitchlords said.

This all started to catch up to me and put me over the edge. I told Hannah I had to get some fresh air and left her there. Probably not the smartest thing to do, but I couldn't take it anymore. I left our home and walked down to the Fours, a local bar/restaurant. A really fun place to be. I walked in and sat down at the bar.

"What can I get you, son?" the bartender asked.

"An extra strong Long Island Iced Tea," I replied.

"You got it." He walked way, made one extra stanky and came back to me.

I didn't even wait for it to be set down on the bar. I took it from his hand and swallowed a huge gulp. I shuddered; it gave me goosebumps. I finished it in record time and ordered another. It hit me slowly, but it was that old familiar feeling that I loved so much. First my stomach started feeling a little warm, then I got slightly light-headed. I started smiling and my thoughts became happy. I suddenly felt talkative, as always happens when I pack on a slight buzz. I turned to the person next to me, who was with a group of people.

"How's it going?" I asked.

"Hey, how are you doing? God bless you," the man replied.

"I don't know if God's blessing me right now honestly, but thank you," I replied.

"God is always good," he said.

"What are you doing here? I asked as I started my second drink.

"We're here protesting a funeral," he said.

I blinked a few times. Didn't say anything. I looked at him and realized he was with the Westboro Baptist Church. Oh God. I took another sip of my drink and my buzz increased. I felt like I could do anything or talk to anyone. How I had missed this feeling.

"Is this about that gay soldier that was killed?" I asked.

"The abomination, you mean?" he said.

"What I don't understand is why you make it your business to hate other people?" I asked.

"It's Biblical, son. The Bible is very clear about what God thinks about homosexuality," he finished.

"But you do realize that it's not a choice, right?" I asked.

"Of course, it's a choice. It's always a choice whether they want to act on their sinful nature or not," he said.

I took another sip. "You know we've had a gay President already, right?" I asked.

"Who?" the man shouted.

"Buchanan. The president right before Lincoln. You know they found love letters that he wrote to people in the White House after he left," I said.

"Sinner all the same," he said.

"You know that they have done FMRI's on LGBT people, and they found that their brains act just like brains of the opposite sex. How can you tell them not to act on their own biology?" I asked.

"Some things aren't fair. Some people are born blind, some deaf. It's how they were born. What matters is how they act," he said.

I wanted to keep going with this dipshit. I swear, smart people sound like crazy people to dumb people. But I looked up and saw white smoke from a chimney. There was a reporter in the Vatican.

"Bartender. Another one please, and turn this up," I said.

"Sure thing," he said.

"In what has been called the fastest and most controversial conclave in history, Pope Aurora Toss I has been elected after the shocking death of Pope Ignatius I. This is a departure from the usual fifteen-day waiting period between death and conclave as the Church's Camerlengo Jean-Louis has stated that the Church is in emergency mode. Something is brewing at the Vatican and who knows when we'll get more answers. From St. Peter's Square, this is Jen Polizzi, signing off."

A new Pope? Could this Pope have been the one that sent Silvio to come find us? I thought about this for a few minutes and came to the conclusion that if they actually knew where the capstones were, they would have removed them by now. The old Pope must have hidden that information from them or destroyed it. I finished my drink and turned to leave. Turned back around and ordered two shots of Jack Honey. Swallowed them, left the bartender a $50 and went outside.

I pushed the door open, and it was still bright out. If there was one thing I hated, it was being drunk in the daytime. I returned to our house and found that nobody was there when I got in. I went to bed and passed out.

Chapter Twenty

I woke up at a quarter to nine the next morning. I had slept for ten hours, and, other than a slight hangover, I felt great. I grabbed a sugar free Red Bull from the kitchen and headed to the living room, rubbing the sleep out of my eyes.

"Um, what exactly do you think you're doing?" Rosette asked sharply.

"Morning ritual. You know I always chug an energy drink when I wake up," I replied.

"Not that, dumbass. What exactly do you think you're doing?" she asked again, this time in a sharper tone.

I looked down and noticed that I was in my boxers. *This isn't what she's talking about, is it? She's seen both of us in our underwear before and that's never bothered her.* "Alright, I'll go put pants on," I said.

"No, you asshole. Did you go out drinking last night?" she asked.

"Did you Graham?" Hannah replied.

Shit. "Look guys, I'm really sorry, but I really couldn't handle last night. Everything just kind of crept up on me and it was a gut reaction what I did," I said.

"Your gut was wrong. Dammit, Newsdon. You were doing so well since you cleaned the house out after NP died. When we needed you the most last night, you were pounding down screwdrivers," she said.

"Actually, they were Long Island Iced Teas," I replied stupidly.

"You know it doesn't fucking matter, right? You're missing the point. We needed you last night, Newsdon, and you let us all down," Rosette said.

She was right. It was a foolish, impulsive thing that I did. I don't know why, but when I see booze, I just can't help myself, and I have to get to the bottom of every bottle. Especially with everything that was going on with us right now, this was not the smartest decision to make.

"Look, I know you're going to be mad for a while. I get that. I screwed up. Big time. I should have been there for both of you. I got scared, I don't know what else to tell you. Ever since James died, things have gotten so much worse to handle," I said.

"Baby, I know. Look, I'm willing to give you the benefit of the doubt this one time, but if it happens again, we're going to have a problem," Hannah said.

"You're right. I'm sorry again. How's Jax?" I asked.

"Twenty-five stitches and a roxy later, he's going to be fine. They're going to let him out soon," Rosette said. I could see the worried look in her eyes. Poor girl.

"Look, we have bigger problems in the meantime. Graham, where's the tube with the writing on it?" Hannah asked.

Oh shit. I had almost forgotten about that. I raced back into our bedroom and pulled it out of the bedside drawer and ran back to the living room with it.

"What does it say?" Rosette asked.

"It's in Italian, guys. What do you want to do? Should we get a translator from Craigslist?" Hannah asked.

"Let's take the second capstone to the vault. I'll think about it on the way there," I said.

We drove to Jean's bank with the vault number and the code, and they let us right in. They asked us how our tall, muscular friend was doing. I could see Rosette clenching her teeth. We put it in the vault. It looked like Rick Ross's safe in there. It reminded me of a story in the Bible. During the time of Sodom and Gomorrah, God made a deal that if there were just a handful of good people in the cities, that they would be spared. They couldn't find any. I believe the number was five good people. All that gambling and prostitution and greed. Lot and Lot's wife had to leave and were instructed not to look back. So, what did she do? She looked back and turned into a pillar of salt. Many people say that was her punishment for looking back. However, during the Roman times people used to get paid a salary which comes from the word Salarium which means salt. Salt was a precious commodity at that time as it preserved food, since there was no refrigeration. So, to read what happened to her another way, she looked back at that decadent place they left and turned into a giant pile of money for all to remember her by. That's what I think of when I think of Jean's fucking safe. We said our goodbyes to the vault and returned to the car.

"Hey Hannah, isn't your cousin Rosa an Italian teacher?" I asked.

"Actually, yes," she replied.

"Want to surprise her after work?" Rosette asked.

"I'll text her and see what she says," Hannah said.

"Just to be safe, we should probably transcribe the message. I don't want to bring her into this by showing her the vial. God knows who knows what it is," I said.

We drove back home, and I got out a pen and pad. I hadn't actually really looked at the vial until now. I slowly wrote down what it said.

Dalle Montagne al Pacifico
La prossima posizione e nella terra conquistata, una fiala data
Fa caldo ma il suo nome non lo e
Questo e in tutti di noi

Alto tanto quanto Christo era vecchio

Dieci metri al rovescio giorno

Il signor Edwards ha il numero del diavolo

Al di dentro della fiala troverai la storia dell' uomo nato dalla seconda roccia

Per curasi il mondo dal 'Drastic Ouijas, hai bisogno di ficlarti del 'Ouija lens'

-I I

"I have no idea what any of that says. I'm guessing Christo is Christ and Pacifico is Pacific?" Hannah asked.

"That's about all I got, too. Oh, and Montagne is Mountain," I replied.

"We've got to get this translated before Jackson gets back," Rosette said.

Hannah received a text inviting her to come by after school let out at three. It was 1:45. We started driving to Weymouth but stopped off at the pier in Hingham to grab some Wahlburgers because they're freakin' delicious. We sat for an hour and talked and laughed, my behavior of the previous night periodically casting a cloud over my good mood. Do better, Graham.

We finished up at Wahlburgers and drove to Weymouth Middle School. We signed in and met Rosa in her classroom, which she shared with a French teacher. He was very pleasant.

"Hello, cousin," Hannah said, as she embraced Rosa.

"Hello to you. Such a delight to see you all here. Graham, it's been how long?" Rosa asked.

"Years. Last time I believe was when we had Thanksgiving dinner together. When James was still around," I said.

"I'm so sorry about that. I've been swamped and meaning to reach out to you. I have three kids now and they drive me insane."

"It's OK," I said. "Listen Rosa, you know why we're here right?" I asked.

"Yes, Hannah filled me in on everything. Where did you get this letter?" she asked.

I shot everyone a look. "It's probably best I don't tell you. I don't want you getting involved."

"Why? Are you in some kind of trouble?" Rosa asked.

"It's just best we not get into it," Rosette said.

We sat down and talked while she took the paper that I wrote out and began by jotting notes. At times she would look up a word on her phone. She was meticulous and wanted to make sure that she has it translated perfectly. After about half an hour, she gave me the paper back. I couldn't believe what I read.

From the Mountains to the Pacific.

The next location will be in the land conquered, a vial provided.

It's hot but its name is not.

This is in all of us. As tall as Jesus was old, 10 meters from the backwards day.

Mr. Edwards has the devil's number.

Within the vial you'll find the tale of the man born of the second stone.

To cure the world of the "Drastic Ouijas," you need to trust the "Ouija Lens."

-I I

"This sounds very interesting. What are you, writing a thriller, Graham?" she joked.

"Um, something like that," I said. "Listen, thanks Rosa, but Rosette's boyfriend is getting back from the hospital, and we really should be home to meet him there," I said.

"Oh, such a shame you can't stay. We're going to Friendly's tonight after laundry," Rosa said, and rolled her eyes.

We laughed and said our goodbyes. Hannah drove home. Well, we'd been right about the Mountains and Pacific and Jesus.

Chapter Twenty-One

We got back to the house and set up a board like NP used to do when we needed to figure things out. After about an hour, there was a knock on our door.

"I'll get it," Hannah said.

She disappeared for a few minutes and then when she came back, she was with Jackson. Rosette squealed in delight.

"How you feeling, big man?" I asked.

"Loopy, but happy to be out of that hellhole. I don't care that Boston has the best hospitals in the country. Still creeps me out to be there," he said.

Jackson never goes to the hospital or doctor. He's in top shape and takes Omegas and nootropics. He's honestly got to be on half the pills that Blur Slanders sells to fund himself. I'd be surprised if he didn't have golden blood.

"So baby, we got this translated. Are you going to help us figure it out?" Rosette asked.

"Yeah, I was looking at the board just now." He looked it over for a minute. "OK, well we know that we are looking for a monolithic statue of some sort? So, we just need to figure out where. The next location will be in the land conquered. Well that's vague. A vial provided. Something in this message is going to tell us what we have to do with that vial. God, this is all so crazy to me guys, what the hell am I doing with myself? I should be writing papers on consciousness being found in microtubules of the brain or teaching grad kids that matter is 99.9% empty space. Not being stabbed and decoding riddles in my free time."

"I'm sorry, bro. Look, if you want to bail, I won't blame you. I'm in too deep right now to get out, but you can still get out if you want," I said.

"Nah, I'm just venting. Let's break down what we know," he said, writing on the board.

From the Mountains to the Pacific – What countries does this span?

The next location will be in the land conquered, a vial provided. - What land? Why isn't a vial provided a separate sentence?

What's hot? What's not?

This is in all of us – Talking about the vial? It's not blood, is it DNA/Serum/White blood cells?

As tall as Jesus was old – So it's either 12 feet tall or 33 feet tall.

10 meters from the backwards day – 30 feet from the night? Possible 30 degrees angle from a constellation?

Mr. Edwards has the devil's number – Who is Mr. Edwards. Why is his number 666

Within the vial you'll find the tale of the man born of the second stone –?

To cure the world of the 'Drastic Ouijas', you need to trust the 'Ouija Lens' - Those words were the same in the Italian letter I see. There's a significance there.

- I I – 2? 11?

We looked at the board for a half an hour until Rosette squealed and jumped up. I hate when she does that. It always scares me.

"It's Chile," she said.

"Actually, it's pretty nice out," I replied.

"No, you tool. The country Chile. It's hot, but it's not. Get it? From the Mountains to the Pacific. From the Andes Mountains to the Pacific Ocean, where Chile is," she said.

"Very possible, but I still think we should look at all other options," Hannah said.

"The next location will be in the land conquered, a vial provided. A vial was provided for us, but 'a vial provided' is also an anagram for Pedro Valdivia, the Spanish conquistador who conquered Chile. It's fucking Chile," Rosette said.

"OK, OK, it's Chile. Wait, when did you get good at anagrams?" I asked.

"Since right now," Rosette said.

"Now what?" Hannah said.

"Well, the last two capstones were under giant hands. So, I looked up monuments in Chile after I figured it out and there happens to be one there. It's as tall as Jesus was old, 33 feet high. Mano de Desierto. Look," she said.

This has to be it, I thought. The last capstone was hidden somewhere under this hand.

"Ten meters from the backwards day? Any idea what that means?" I asked.

"No clue, but we have to go there and figure it out. I'm booking us a flight in two days to Antofagasta. It's only about an hour drive from the monument. I even found instructions on how to get there," Rosette said.

I was really impressed by her at this point. She was showing signs of NP's brilliance.

"OK, that works for us, but we still have to figure out what the rest of the letter says," I said.

"What does 'this is in all of us' mean?" Jackson asked.

"Maybe it has to do with the vial provided?" Hannah asked.

Of course! Why didn't I think of that? Actually, I had, but I was stumped and couldn't figure out exactly what liquid was there and what we are supposed to do with it.

"I'm starving," Hannah said.

We went out to grab some dinner at Chili's. We continued talking about the letter over dinner, but quietly enough that people around us couldn't hear us. People were already after us and we couldn't take any chances. Finally, Hannah had a breakthrough.

"Within the vial you'll find the tale of the man born of the second stone. The second capstone. There's information in this vial coded somehow that has to do with a man born in the Canary Islands," Hannah said.

All at once it hit me like a ton of bricks. I thought back to when we figured out that my brother had left a coded message inside a crystal. That had been pretty cutting edge at the time. But I recently learned about how people were able to store information in DNA and retrieve it later. See with micro and nano chips, eventually you run out of space. In crystals, although the technology is still very young, the same will happen as well. But if you were to compress all of history and everything we know into DNA, it could fit within a few cubic centimeters. This is what he must have meant when he said, "This is in all of us." It's DNA.

"Guys we have to head home right now, I can't talk about it here, but I know what we have to do," I said.

Back at the house, I sat them all down and explained my train of thought to them, and how I knew what had happened. I even showed them the vial. The slightly milky substance was the DNA floating around in there.

"So, what's our next move, Newsdon?" Rosette asked.

I picked up the phone and dialed the only person I could think of that could possibly know what to do: Conrad at Senna Ore. He was helpful before, and, when he picked up, he was really happy to hear from me. He said he had been wondering if I would ever contact him again. He asked me how Jean looked when I went to see him, and we discussed that. Most importantly though, he explained how he would be able to help as he was already two steps ahead of us.

It seemed his forte was cutting edge experiments. We had to see him at noon the next day. It wouldn't take long to extract the information, and he would grant us the family discount again, but the one thing we needed to figure out was where on the DNA it was. Without that bit of knowledge there was no way they would be able to locate the information. I was about to tell him to look for the Canary Islands in it, but he stopped me and told me not to say anything on the phone. What he was doing was technically off the books.

We said our goodbyes and I sent Jackson and Rosette back home to Chestnut Hill to pack. We were going to take a late-night road trip and spend the night at Goat Island again so we could be at Conrad's lab first thing in the morning. Now the only problem was, how the hell were we going to figure out where the information on the DNA was hiding?

How is it possible that everybody is always born into the correct religion? - Ricky Gervais

Chapter Twenty-Two

"Morning, sunshines," I said, as I woke them all up at nine and opened the curtain to show our gorgeous view of the water. Honestly, I could get used to living like this. "Time for coffee or Red Bull or whatever. We have to be there by eleven and it's a half hour drive. Plus, it takes like twenty minutes to get your car out of this place."

"Can't we sleep a little longer?" Rosette whined.

We drove through the night to get there, so I could understand why everybody was a little cranky. "No time for laziness, Rose. Get your ass up," I said.

"Alright, we're up," Jackson said, wincing a little. He must have still been in pain from that pesky stabbing incident.

"You need to take a Percocet or something, Jax?" I asked.

"Nah man, I'm straight. If I do need something, I'll take it after our meeting today. I don't want to be zoned out or sleeping in a corner. This shit is super cool," he said.

We showered and dressed, packed and got in the car. The weather was crisp and cool. Nice day for an adventure. We drove to Senna Ore, making a pit stop at Dunkin' Donuts for coffee. Did you know that the first Dunkin' Donuts was in Boston? I learned that from the drive-thru lady.

Conrad met us outside. After some fresh introductions we went inside.

The lab looked completely different this time around. It looked like a CDC outpost. Like every *Resident Evil* movie. These scientists were not joking around. I showed him the vial.

"OK, guys. Where are we looking for this message and what are we looking for?" Conrad asked.

A small wave of panic rushed over me, but I buried it deep inside, as calm as a surgeon. "We don't exactly know yet," I said.

"Well that's unfortunate. First, let's make sure this is what we think it is and we'll take it from there," Conrad said, as he waved over one of the other scientists, who was wearing goggles and gloves and a full-body white suit. "This is Dr. Pivarnick. He's a geneticist and our lead extractor. Believe it or not, this business can be very profitable. I need to run for a minute, I'll leave this with him and see if we are able to help," he said, and walked away.

Dr. Pivarnick went into the lab and started working on the samples. It was all way over my head, I wish I knew what he was doing. After about twenty minutes, he turned and gave us a thumbs-up. So, this was DNA and I was right. Now what?

Frustrated, we went outside, and I grabbed a cigarette from an old pack in the car. I stress smoke sometimes. I walked back behind the building where everyone else was.

"The sperm decides the gender," Hannah said.

"I'm not arguing that point with you, what I'm saying is that research shows that, although the sperm decides the gender, the egg decides which sperm it will allow in," Rosette said.

"What are you girls talking about?" I asked.

"Sperm and eggs. You want in?" Rosette asked.

"Wait, neither of you are pregnant, are you?" I asked, slightly horrified.

"No, dumbass," Rosette said.

"Good, because now's not the time or the place," I said.

"I'm cool with that," Jackson said.

As we sat outside and talked, Dr. Pivarnick came outside and lit up a cigarette.

"Mr. Edwards has the devil's number," Rosette said. "What's so special about 666?" she asked.

"It's the sign of the man. Carbon. Sixth element, six protons and six neutrons. The mark of the beast is man," Jackson said.

"That can't be it. Maybe you multiply them together. Does 216 mean anything?" Hannah asked.

"I can't think of anything," Rosette replied.

"Well, what about adding them together. Eighteen. Could that mean anything?" I asked.

"Well, in the Jewish religion," Rosette started.

"We know all about this. We went through it already. It can't be the same thing. Ugh, this is so frustrating," I said. I turned to Dr. Pivarnick. "Hey doc, care to help us out with a riddle?" I asked.

"I'll try. Lay it on me," he said.

"Mr. Edwards has the Devil's number," I said. "The numbers are six, 216 or eighteen. Does any of this make any sense to you?"

Pivarnick sat there puffing on his cigarette for a minute and I could see a light bulb light up in his head. Then he looked disappointed. He kept smoking.

"What?" I asked.

"It's probably nothing. I'm a geneticist by nature and I see patterns in my work the way you see patterns in your life. The devil's number is triple six. Triple six is eighteen. Three copies of the eighteenth chromosome is something called Edwards syndrome," he said, as he looked like he was starting to get some more life in him. "It's worth a shot looking for it. What are we looking for exactly?" he said.

"Something about the Canary Islands," I said. Shit, this was as good a shot as anything else.

We all went inside and Dr. Pivarnick went back to work on the eighteenth chromosome. At least he didn't have to filter through all the others. After about an hour and a half of him working and us talking and trying to figure out what the backwards day was, he tapped on the glass to summon us. He had sequenced something and was extracting it as he spoke to us. This was a very long story, he said, but we were right about the Canary Islands. This story was about a former priest named Alberto Rivera who was born in Las Palmas, Canary Islands. His story was going to change the way I thought about everything.

Chapter Twenty-Three

We said our goodbyes to Conrad and Dr. Pivarnick. Dr. Pivarnick handed me a flash drive with the information extracted from the DNA. My hands were shaking as I took it. I didn't want to tell everyone what I had found out until we got home. It was better this way.

The drive home was uneventful. Aside from a little bit of traffic, it only took about two hours to get back from Rhode Island to Quincy. We entered the house and Jackson disarmed the trip wire that he had put in, in the event someone tried to break in. You can never be too careful these days. I grabbed my laptop and plugged in the flash drive, connecting a projector via the other USB link. The living room wall lit up like a movie screen.

"OK, guys. I've read some of this and it's real heavy. If you feel that you cannot handle this, then feel free to leave right now. Once you read this, you won't be able to unlearn it," I said.

"Just get on with it already," Rosette said.

I opened the file. Here is what we read.

What I'm going to tell you is what I learned in secret briefings in the Vatican when I was a Jesuit priest, under oath and induction.

A Jesuit cardinal named Augustine Bea showed us how desperately the Roman Catholics wanted Jerusalem at the end of the third century.

Because of its religious history and its strategic location, the Holy City was considered a priceless treasure. A scheme had to be developed to make Jerusalem a Roman Catholic city.

The great untapped source of manpower that could do this job was the children of Ishmael. The poor Arabs fell victim to one of the most clever plans ever devised by the powers of darkness.

Early Christians went everywhere spreading the gospel and setting up small churches, but they met heavy opposition. Both the Jews and the Roman government persecuted the believers in Christ to stop their spread. But the Jews rebelled against Rome, and in 70 AD, Roman armies under General Titus smashed Jerusalem and destroyed the great Jewish temple which was the heart of Jewish worship in fulfillment of Christ's prophecy in Matthew 24:2.

The Dome of the Rock Mosque stands today on this holy place where the temple once stood, as Islam's second most holy place.

Sweeping changes were in the wind. Corruption, apathy, greed, cruelty, perversion and rebellion were eating at the Roman Empire, and it was ready to collapse.

The persecution against Christians was useless, as they continued to lay down their lives for the gospel of Christ.

The only way Satan could stop this thrust was to create a counterfeit "Christian" religion to destroy the work of God. The solution was in Rome. Their religion had come from ancient Babylon and all it needed was a facelift. This didn't happen overnight but began in the writings of the "early church fathers."

It was through their writings that a new religion would take shape. The statue of Jupiter in Rome was eventually called St. Peter, and the statue of Venus was changed to the Virgin Mary. The site chosen for its headquarters was on one of the seven hills called "Vaticanus," the place of diving serpents where the Satanic temple of Janus stood.

The great counterfeit religion was Roman Catholicism, called "Mystery, Babylon the Great, the Mother of Harlots and Abominations of the Earth." Revelation 17:5. She was raised up to block the gospel, slaughter the believers in Christ, establish religions, create wars and make the nations drunk with the wine of her fornication, as we will see.

The three major monotheistic religions have one thing in common: each has a holy place where they look for guidance. Roman Catholicism looks to the Vatican as the Holy City. The Jews look to the wailing wall in Jerusalem, and the Muslims look to Mecca as their Holy City. Each group believes that they receive certain types of blessings for the rest of their lives for visiting their holy place.

In the beginning, Arab visitors would bring gifts to the "House of God," and the keepers of the Kaaba were gracious to all who came. Some brought their idols and they were placed inside the sanctuary, in order not to offend these people. It is said that the Jews looked upon the Kaaba as an outlying tabernacle of the Lord, with veneration, until it became polluted with idols.

In a tribal contention over a well—Zamzam—the treasure of the Kaaba and the offerings that pilgrims had given were dumped down the well and it was filled with sand; it disappeared. Many years later, Adb Al-Muttalib was given visions telling him where to find the well and its treasure. He became the hero of Mecca, and he was destined to become the grandfather of Muhammad.

Before this time, Augustine became the bishop of North Africa and was effective in winning Arabs to Roman Catholicism, including whole tribes. It was among these Arab converts to Catholicism that the concept of looking for an Arab prophet developed.

Muhammad's father died from illness and sons born to great Arab families in places like Mecca were sent into the desert to be suckled and weaned and spend some of their childhood with Bedouin tribes for training and to avoid the plagues in the cities.

After his mother and grandfather also died, Muhammad was with his uncle when a Roman Catholic monk learned of his identity and said, "Take your brother's son back to his country and guard him against the Jews, for by God, if they see him and know of him that which I know, they will construe evil against him. Great things are in store for this brother's son of yours."

The Roman Catholic monk had fanned the flames for future Jewish persecutions at the hands of the followers of Muhammad. The Vatican desperately wanted Jerusalem because of its religious significance but was blocked by the Jews.

Another problem was the true Christians in North Africa who preached the gospel. Roman Catholicism was growing in power but would not tolerate opposition.

Somehow the Vatican had to create a weapon to eliminate both the Jews and the true Christian believers who refused to accept Roman Catholicism. Looking to North Africa, they saw the multitudes of Arabs as a source of manpower to do their dirty work.

Some Arabs had become Roman Catholic and could be used to report information to leaders in Rome. Others were part of an underground spy network carrying out

Rome's master plan to control the great multitudes of Arabs who rejected Catholicism. When "St. Augustine" appeared on the scene, he knew what was going on. His monasteries served as bases to seek out and destroy Bible manuscripts owned by the true Christians.

The Vatican wanted to create a messiah for the Arabs, someone they could raise up as a great leader, a man with charisma whom they could train, eventually uniting all the non-Catholic Arabs behind him, creating a mighty army that would ultimately capture Jerusalem for the pope.

In the Vatican briefing, Cardinal Bea told us this story:

"A wealthy Arabian lady who was a faithful follower of the Pope played a tremendous part in this drama. She was a widow named Khadijah. She gave her wealth to the church and retired to a convent but was given an assignment. She was to find a brilliant young man who could be used by the Vatican to create a new religion and become the messiah for the children of Ishmael.

"Khadijah had a cousin named Waraquah, who was also a very faithful Roman Catholic, and the Vatican placed him in a critical role as Muhammad's advisor. He had tremendous influence on Muhammad.

"Teachers were sent to young Muhammad and he had intensive training. Muhammad studied the works of

St. Augustine which prepared him for his 'great calling'. The Vatican had Catholic Arabs across North Africa spread the story of a great one who was about to rise up among the people and be the chosen one of their God.

"While Muhammad was being prepared, he was told that his enemies were the Jews and that the only true Christians were Roman Catholic. He was taught that others calling themselves Christians were actually wicked impostors and should be destroyed. Many Muslims believed this.

"Muhammad began receiving 'divine revelations' and his wife's Catholic cousin Waraquah helped interpret them. From this came the Koran. In the fifth year of Muhammad's mission, persecution came against his followers because they refused to worship the idols in the Kaaba.

"Muhammad instructed some of them to flee to Abysinnia where Negus, the Roman Catholic king accepted them because Muhammad's views on the virgin Mary were so close to Roman Catholic doctrine. These Muslims received protection from Catholic kings because of Muhammad's revelations.

"Muhammad later conquered Mecca and the Kaaba was cleared of idols. History proves that before Islam came into existence, the Sabeans in Arabia worshiped the moon-god who was married to the sun-god. They

gave birth to three goddesses who were worshipped throughout the Arab world as 'Daughters of Allah'. An idol excavated at Hazor in Palestine in the 1950s shows Allah sitting on a throne with the crescent moon on his chest.

"Muhammad claimed he had a vision from Allah and was told, 'You are the messenger of Allah'. This began his career as a prophet, and he received many messages. By the time Muhammad died, the religion of Islam was exploding. The nomadic Arab tribes were joining forces in the name of Allah and his prophet, Muhammad.

"Some of Muhammad's writings were placed in the Koran, others were never published. They are now in the hands of high-ranking holy men (Ayatollahs) in the Islamic faith."

When Cardinal Bea shared this with us in the Vatican, he said, "These writings are guarded because they contain information that link the Vatican to the creation of Islam. Both sides have so much information on each other that, if it was exposed, it could create a scandal that would be a disaster for both religions."

In their "holy" book, the Koran, Christ is regarded as only a prophet. If the Pope was His representative on earth, then he also must be a prophet of God. This caused the followers of Muhammad to fear and respect the Pope as another "holy man".

The Pope moved quickly and issued bulls granting the Arab generals permission to invade and conquer the nations of North Africa. The Vatican helped to finance the building of these massive Islamic armies in exchange for three favors:

1. Eliminate the Jews and Christians (true believers, which they called infidels).

2. Protect the Augustinian Monks and Roman Catholics.

3. Conquer Jerusalem for "His Holiness" in the Vatican.

As time went by, Islam's power became tremendous. Jews and true Christians were slaughtered, and Jerusalem fell into their hands. Roman Catholics were never attacked, nor were their shrines, during this time. But when the Pope asked for Jerusalem, he was surprised at their refusal! The Arab generals had achieved such military success that they could not be intimidated by the Pope; nothing could stand in the way of their own plan.

Under Waraquah's direction, Muhammad wrote that Abraham offered Ishmael as a sacrifice. The Bible says that Isaac was the sacrifice, but Muhammad removed Isaac's name and inserted Ishmael's name. As a result of this and Muhammad's vision, the faithful Muslims built a mosque, the Dome of the Rock, in Ishmael's honor on the site of the Jewish temple that was destroyed in 70

AD. This made Jerusalem the second most holy place in the Muslim faith. How could they give such a sacred shrine to the Pope without causing a revolt?

The Pope realized what they had created was out of control when he heard they were calling "His Holiness" an infidel. The Muslim generals were determined to conquer the world for Allah, and now they turned toward Europe. Islamic ambassadors approached the Pope and asked for papal bulls to give them permission to invade European countries.

The Vatican was outraged; war was inevitable. Temporal power and control of the world was considered a basic right of the Pope. He wouldn't think of sharing it with those whom he considered heathens.

The Pope raised up his armies and called them crusades to hold back the children of Ishmael from grabbing Catholic Europe. The Crusades lasted centuries and Jerusalem slipped out of the Pope's hands.

Turkey fell and Spain and Portugal were invaded by Islamic forces. In Portugal, they called a mountain village "Fatima" in honor of Muhammad's daughter, never dreaming it would become world famous.

Years later when the Muslim armies were poised to invade Italy from the islands of Sardinia and Corsica, there was a serious problem. The Islamic generals realized they were overextended. It was time for peace talks. One of the negotiators was Francis of Assisi.

As a result, the Muslims were allowed to occupy Turkey in a "Christian" world, and the Catholics were allowed to occupy Lebanon in the Arab world.

It was also agreed that the Muslims could build mosques in Catholic countries without interference as long as Roman Catholicism could flourish in Arab countries.

Cardinal Bea told us in Vatican briefings that both the Muslims and Roman Catholics agreed to block and destroy the efforts of their common enemy, Bible-believing Christian missionaries. Through these concordats, Satan blocked the children of Ishmael from a knowledge of Scripture and the truth.

A light control was kept on Muslims from the Ayatollah down through the Islamic priests, nuns and monks. The Vatican also engineers a campaign of hatred between the Muslim Arabs and the Jews. Before this, they had co-existed peacefully.

The Islamic community looks on the Bible-believing missionary as a devil who brings poison to the children of Allah. This explains years of ministry in those countries with little results.

The next plan was to control Islam. In 1910, Portugal was going socialist. Red flags were appearing, and the

Catholic Church was facing a major problem. Increasing numbers were against the church.

The Jesuits wanted Russia involved, and the location of this vision at Fatima could play a key part in pulling Islam to the Mother Church.

In 1917, the Virgin appeared in Fatima. "The Mother of God" was a smashing success, playing to overflow crowds. As a result, the Socialists of Portugal suffered a major defeat.

Roman Catholics worldwide began praying for the conversion of Russia, and the Jesuits invented the Novenas to Fatima which they could perform throughout North Africa, spreading good public relations to the Muslim world. The Arabs thought they were honoring the daughter of Muhammad, which is what the Jesuits wanted them to believe.

As a result of the vision of Fatima, Pope Pius XII ordered his Nazi army to crush Russia and the Orthodox religion and make Russia Roman Catholic. A few years after he lost World War II, Pope Pius XII startled the world with his phony "dancing Sun" vision to keep Fatima in the news. It was great religious show biz and the world swallowed it.

Not surprisingly, Pope Pius was the only one to see this vision.

As a result, a group of followers has grown into a Blue Army worldwide, totaling millions of faithful Roman Catholics ready to die for the Blessed Virgin. But we haven't seen anything yet. The Jesuits have their Virgin Mary scheduled to appear four or five times in China, Russia, and major appearance in the U.S.

What has this got to do with Islam?

Note Bishop Fulton Sheen's statement:

"Our Lady's appearances at Fatima marked the turning point in the history of the world's 350 million Muslims. After the death of his daughter, Muhammad wrote that she 'is the most holy of all women in Paradise, next to Mary.'"

He believed that the Virgin Mary chose to be known as Our Lady of Fatima as a sign and a pledge that the Muslims who believe in Christ's virgin birth will come to believe in his divinity.

Bishop Sheen pointed out that the pilgrim virgin statues of Our Lady of Fatima were enthusiastically received by Muslims in Africa, India, and elsewhere, and that many Muslims are now coming into the Roman Catholic Church.

This came from a book written by Jesuit priest Alberto Rivera before he was poisoned. The book has since been removed from circulation, and many websites have tried to smear his name. Thinking back to this, it all made sense, though. Finally, I spoke up.

"It's interesting isn't it? During Taurus, the Egyptians were the dominant culture. The Jews were rising, but it was still Egyptian. Then the Egyptian culture started to die out in Aries and the Jews started becoming more prominent. Then the Jewish culture started to die down in Pisces, when the Christian culture took over. Islam started at the midpoint of Pisces and now we see in Aquarius that Christianity is starting to die down and Islam is the new dominant culture. It seems that there is always a dominant culture in every single Zodiac sign. Who knows what's going to happen now with this new Pope Aurora Toss I. Aurora like Aurora Borealis and Toss like throw it out. As if he's sending a message against astrology."

I could see on their faces that they had never thought of that before. What had we just read? This secret would destroy two of the world's major religions. Who would have access to this? It had to be the Pope; I, I at the end of the letter on the vial had to stand for Ignatius the First. I shared this with them, and they agreed. A mysterious death and a buried secret that could be bigger than what I thought at the time was the world's deepest secret.

"What are we going to do with this?" Jackson asked.

I knew what I wanted to do, but I had to run it by them first. This was going to put our lives in jeopardy, but I got the sense from everyone that they understood it was bigger than us.

"I'm going to AquaStream this to my followers. I'm not sure if we're going to make it out alive, and I need to know that this information was put out in the open," I said. It blew my mind after all this that we still had one capstone remaining. God only knew what secret that would unveil. I had Jackson shoot the video.

"Hello, everybody. I know it's been a while since I've been on here, but I've been busy. What I'm about to tell you could get me killed. But it's worth it. We've already had a man named Silvio Bruno come to my house from the Vatican and try. If it was me, I probably would be dead by now. But he confronted my good friend Jackson instead who was able to overpower him. Silvio was a hit man for the Vatican. There's a lot going on behind the scenes that you don't know about, and there will always be trolls. But you all don't have a complete picture of what happened. So, let me start from the beginning. It all started with a call from my mother telling me that my brother had died in the war."

Chapter Twenty-Four

Out of breath and shaking, the Camerlengo ran to see the Pope, who was in his chambers. He calmed himself down and popped a Xanax. This would take about fifty minutes to hit. He had timed how fast they kicked in both with and without food. He was taking them like candy at this point.

"What is it, Camerlengo?" The Pope asked.

"There is a video that went online a few hours ago. You have to see this," the Camerlengo said.

The Camerlengo pulled up Graham Newsdon's video which was going viral. It had nearly two million hits at this point, and it had only been five hours. He sat while the Pope watched; he could see the other man's face turn blood red and a vein pop in his forehead. He looked worried, then angry again.

"Nobody is going to believe this story. This was the kid with the dead brother that got into it with the US President, isn't it?" the Pope asked.

The Camerlengo nodded.

"Call a meeting of the cardinals. Your sole duty until further notice, Camerlengo, is to follow up with this. Until I say otherwise," the Pope said.

"Yes, Your Holiness," Jean-Louis replied.

He rounded up all the cardinals and brought them to Chiesa parrocchiale di Sant'Anna dei Palafrenieri. The Pope would have wanted to keep the meeting low-key. He didn't like doing business in St. Peter's Basilica. After a few minutes of murmurs and whispers, the Pope arrived.

"Brothers, I have no time to waste so I'm going to get right to it. Silvio is dead," the Pope said. There were gasps in the crowd.

"What happened?" Cardinal Sorrentino asked.

"We sent him to take care of that American kid that has been such a problem to us. While he was there, he went to his house. He wasn't home, but somebody much bigger and stronger was. There was a struggle and he ended up on his own knife," the Pope said.

"How do you know all of this?" said Cardinal DelVecchio.

"Camerlengo, if you will," the Pope said.

The Camerlengo connected his private phone to an old TV in the Church. Soon the screen flickered. He went to AquaStream and played the video for the cardinals. It lasted about twenty minutes, but it encapsulated everything that Graham had gone through up to that point. There were audible gasps in the crowd. Finally, the video ended and the Camerlengo turned the TV off.

"What are we going to do?" asked Cardinal Sorrentino.

"For starters, I've sent a team to take care of him, his girlfriend and his friends. This time tomorrow they should be dead. Well, not Graham. We have something planned for him. Then we can start spinning the story," the Pope said.

"But what about the part about Alberto Rivera?" asked Cardinal DelVecchio.

"What about him? The internet already says he's a crazy conspiracy nut. Plus, we know for a fact that Graham is an alcoholic who couldn't handle the death of his brother. Soon he won't be able to handle the death of his girlfriend and best friends and will spiral down until he takes his own life, just like his brother. I've sent Vincent and his team," the Pope said.

"Is it true? Is what he said about Rivera true?" Cardinal Sorrentino asked.

The Pope looked directly into his eyes and asked, "Does it matter if it is?"

"But what about the capstones?" asked Cardinal Sorrentino.

"That is the problem. It seems that our dearly departed Pope Ignatius had secretly distributed them without our knowledge. From the video we know that they have two of them. I'm hoping that Vincent and his team can get their work done before they find the third, and then it can be lost forever," the Pope said.

Some of the cardinals, especially Cardinal Sorrentino, did not take too kindly to the phrase "dearly departed." He found it to be shallow and disrespectful. Things had not been sitting well with that cardinal ever since Aurelio took the helm. He was just going to be silent until his time came, and he could do something.

"What exactly happens when all three capstones are replaced?" Cardinal Sorrentino asked.

"I have no idea," said the Pope. In truth, he knew exactly what was going to happen and it scared the daylights out of him. If the astrological revelations didn't bring the Church down, if the now released Alberto Rivera information didn't either, then this most certainly would. There was a lot on the line for him.

Chapter Twenty-Five

We were all still packed from our trip to Rhode Island, so we figured we would just hang out and relax until our flight. It was still bothering us that we couldn't figure out what the backwards day meant. Or that Ouija phrase. The dead Pope had left them there for someone to figure out, and it was driving us crazy. Blur Slanders was on TV now, and he was talking about Operation Blue Beam, a declassified operation that asserted that at one point the government wanted to project the image of Jesus in the sky, or Muhammad, in order to get people under mass control. Hell, if the Virgin Mary on toast was something, imagine millions of people looking to the sky and seeing their prophet. I couldn't listen to this anymore. I turned the TV off.

"Hey guys, I'm going down the block to pick up some cigarettes. I'll be back," I said.

I walked to the corner store, where I bought a pack of cigarettes and then started walking back home. All at once I heard tires screech and a door open, and someone put a bag over my head. Then I felt a hard blow, and suddenly everything went dark.

I awoke in what I can only assume was a few hours later, bag still on my head.

"I think he's awake," someone said.

"Good, it's about time. How hard did you hit the kid?"

I heard footsteps and somebody took the bag off my head. I squinted my eyes as I could see the sun. My wrists and ankles were zip-tied to a chair, I was in my boxers and there were shipping containers and 55-gallon drums everywhere. *Shit, I must be at the Seaport*, I thought. *Who are these characters now?*

One of them came slowly up to me, smoking a cigarette.

"You're Graham Newsdon, right?" he asked. I didn't say anything. Suddenly he turned his hand around and backhanded me in the face. Shit, that was going to leave a mark. I could already feel my left eye swelling up.

"Let's try this again. You're Graham Newsdon, right?" he asked again.

I didn't say anything again. When I saw him clench his fist, I spoke, "It'd be a pretty big shame if I wasn't, at this point of our relationship, right?"

"Wiseass. Keep it coming, kid. You have no idea what you've gotten yourself into," he said.

I turned my head as much as I could and looked around. Yup, I was pretty much isolated and pretty much fucked. This didn't look too good for me.

"Who are you?" I asked.

"Who do you think we are?" he said.

"Well, let's see. You must work for the same people that sent over that big dead guy, right?" I said.

They didn't like that one bit. The big guy smacked me again, in the same spot. I turned and spit blood onto the floor.

"If I had to guess, you're here on behalf of that new Pope that we love so much, right?" I asked.

"You're too smart for your own good, kid. One day it's going to get you killed," the big guy said.

"One day? So, you're not here to kill me?"

"Not at all," the big guy said. "Your video has made you too high profile to kill." He leaned forward, looking me in my good eye. "So, here's what we're going to do. We're going to kill your girlfriend, then your friends in your house. But not before we set up a story that you lost your mind. Nobody is going to believe that video you sent out at that point, and you'll eventually take your own life, just like your brother did. We'll blame it on the Blue Whale Challenge or something like that," he said, and grinned.

"You son of a bitch!" I said.

"Whoa there, take it easy. I said we're not going to kill you. We're just going to have fun with you, a lot of it. Then we are going to let you on your merry way.

There's a van heading to your house as we speak. Now. Any last words before we get started?"

I didn't say anything.

"Do you want to tell us where the last capstone is?" he asked.

It never occurred to me that they didn't know. Ignatius must have destroyed all the evidence of where they were hidden before his death. This was the one thing I could possibly use as leverage.

"Want to come look for it with me?" I asked and flashed a bloody smile.

They cut the zip ties and one of them hit me in the face again. They picked up my slumped body from the ground and placed me inside an oil drum with a piece of the lid cut off. It was filled neck deep with liquid. They put the lid on top. This was water, not oil, so that was good. *Always look on the positive side of things, Graham*, I thought. *God, I could really use a drink. This is pure MK Ultra. Sensory deprivation. They are going to keep me in this for days, probably only letting me out to eat slightly then put me back in. Throughout the night they'll probably bang on the drum to make sure I'm awake.*

I was in the drum for about twenty minutes when I heard a body hit the floor. Everything echoed in there.

"Hey, what are you doing here?" I heard one of them say and then another thud. Finally, I heard a scuffle and the sound of body parts slapping on the cold hard floor. Then it went silent. I sat there completely still for some reason until I heard the lid starting to unscrew. I looked up squinting, as I had been in the dark for about half an hour, and to my surprise I saw Jackson!

"You OK, man?" he asked. "Damn, they fucked you up, didn't they?

"I'll be fine," I said as he helped me out of the tank. I found my pants on the floor and my shirt completely ripped. He gave me his shirt; he had a tank top under it. Did I mention how huge this guy was?

"What did they say?" he asked.

"We have to get back to the house," I said. "They're sending a team to come and get the girls," I said as I started coughing up water.

"Well they're not going to find them there, they're at the airport already. Which is where we're headed if you're still up to it," he said.

"Jackson, they have no idea where we're going," I said.

"I know kid, I heard the whole thing," he said.

"Just out of curiosity, how the hell did you find me?" I asked.

"I came outside to tell you that there was a pack of cigarettes in the house, and you weren't there. You must have been in the store. I saw you walk out and them jump you. I ducked behind the big SUV that parks in front of your house and hopped on my motorcycle and followed them here," he said.

"But how did you take them out?" I said, as I examined the carnage.

"With this." He showed what looked like a pair of brass knuckles. "I gave this to Rosette so she'll be fine when she walks home late from swim meets," he said.

"Brass knuckles?" I asked.

"Kinda," he said, as he flicked a switch on the side and a blue burst of electricity started running back and forth between the top two knuckles.

"It's a taser too?" I asked, surprised.

"Yup. How do you think I took out those two?" He pointed to the two lying by the van.

"Well, what about that guy?" I pointed to the man passed out next to the drum I was just rescued from.

"Oh him? Nah, I just beat the shit out of him," Jackson said.

"Oh. Well, OK then," I said. "I wonder what it feels like being tasered by that."

He looked at me cockeyed for a moment. "Graham, this is why you can't have nice things," he laughed. "Chile?" he asked.

"Chile," I said.

We grabbed the goons one by one and shut them in a cargo shipping container after we zip-tied them to pieces of cargo. If the heat wasn't going to kill them, maybe they could enjoy a nice trip across the ocean.

We hopped onto the back of his motorcycle and got the hell out of there. We had a flight to catch.

Chapter Twenty-Six

Furious, the Pope burst into the Camerlengo's quarters. "He got away again!"

"What?" the Camerlengo replied.

"I just got off the phone with Vincent. Apparently, his friend followed them with a taser and locked them all in a shipping container. I could hear the sound of the giant boat horn as they were being sent God knows where. Goddammit!" the Pope said.

The Camerlengo couldn't believe the Pope just used the Lord's name in vain. He already disliked him and had issues in the past, but this was pushing it. He was beginning to wonder if the Pope had fought his way to his position just so he could take these kids out. Honestly, Jean-Louis was impressed that the kids had been able to fight them off this long.

"And we don't even know where they are going," the Pope fumed.

"What would you have me do, Your Holiness?" the Camerlengo asked.

"Call another meeting. I'll meet you there in twenty minutes," the Pope said.

The Camerlengo smiled as the Pope left. He was secretly rooting for these kids at this point. He was convinced that his great friend was murdered, and that this new Pope was the root of all evil. Nevertheless, he did as he was told and gathered everyone into the Church again. After twenty minutes, the Pope walked in.

"Brothers, once again our team has failed us," the Pope began. "I don't understand. The Swiss Guard has protected us for generations. Yet they can't take out four pesky kids. I have no idea where they are. But that is why I wanted to call you here," the Pope said as he took a deep breath. This was going to be the tricky part. "I've called Russell in to help," he said, to audible gasps.

"Your Holiness, this is highly unorthodox," said Cardinal Sorrentino.

"Fuck orthodox. I'm tired of these kids. Have their passports flagged!" the Pope shouted. Some of the cardinals were beginning to become uncomfortable.

"We can't. We don't have that authority to do that. Technically they haven't broken any laws in their country," Cardinal DelVecchio said.

"Well, somebody's got to do something! Any suggestions?" he asked. There was only silence. "Nobody has anything to say? This is your livelihood that's at stake here. It's all our livelihoods. Dammit, where's Russell?" he asked.

"He's twenty minutes away. There was some traffic," the Camerlengo said.

"Well, tell him to hurry," the Pope lambasted.

The Pope slumped into a chair. The cardinals began to murmur among themselves. They had never seen so much disorder come from the papacy in their lives, and many of them were nearing 80. They sat there with the Pope for a half an hour until some started shuffling, getting ready to leave.

"Where are you all headed? You're not going anywhere. I want you all witness to this at this point," he said.

A few minutes later a tall middle-aged gentleman walked through the church doors with a friendly smile for the assembled cardinals. He was wearing a button-down shirt tucked into jeans with a blazer over it and a fedora. When he smiled, the wrinkles in his face made him seem older than he was. The Camerlengo smiled back at him, not knowing what to think. What was about to happen was as close to voodoo as any of them had ever seen.

"Gentlemen. Do you know why I am here?" Russell asked. Some nodded and others shook their heads no.

"Do you believe that what I do is of the Devil?" he asked. Again, some nodded and some shook their heads.

"What is the purpose to all of this?" asked Cardinal Sorrentino.

"Simple," Russell said. "We're going to gain access and find out where these kids have gone, and you are going to send people after them. Does that about summarize it?"

Again, some nodded. Others, like the Camerlengo, were sweating. This entire conclave had been unreformed, unorthodox and completely out of line with what the Church stood for and what it was supposed to do.

"Alright, let's get started," Russell said and closed his eyes.

"What is he doing exactly?" Cardinal Sorrentino asked the Camerlengo.

"Remote viewing," Jean-Louis said. He couldn't believe he was saying that out loud.

"I need quiet to do this, please," Russell said.

They sat in the sweltering heat for half an hour while Russell closed his eyes and swayed. It was a pretty good dramatic performance, the Camerlengo thought, but this was not going to help find them. He didn't even know if he wanted them found anymore.

After another few minutes, Russell started to speak. "I see a house, next door to a nail salon and massage parlor," he began. "I see a Chinese, no, a pizza place across the street." He bobbed and swayed. "I see the house clear as day. I'm looking in the window now. Nobody is home," he said.

"Obviously nobody is home, we are trying to find out where they are!" the Pope raged.

"Please remain quiet or I'll lose my connection," Russell said. He stood silently for another few minutes. Finally, he spoke up again.

"The front door is locked, but there is a back entrance up three flights of stairs on a shoddy wooden staircase," he said. "The window was left open a crack." A few more minutes of silence passed, until he yelled and startled the entire room.

"I'm in the house!" he said. For the next few minutes, he supposedly glided from room to room, looking in drawers.

The Camerlengo was getting bored. He looked at his watch and realized he had missed his last Xanax. Oddly, he didn't feel like he needed one. *This could be the beginning of something special*, he thought.

Finally, Russell spoke up again. "I see a TV in the living room. There is some kind of talk show on it. I see cans of energy drinks on the kitchen table," he said.

"Come on already. Give us something we can use," the Pope said.

"I see mail on the table. I see clothes on the couch. Wait. I see a laptop on the couch. Let me try and see what's on it," he said. He cocked his head as if playing a virtual reality game and shut his eyes even tighter.

"There is a flight itinerary on the computer," he said.

Seemingly more excited than he'd ever been in his life, the Pope said, "What's it say?"

"Chile. More specifically, a flight to Santiago and then a connecting flight to Antofagasta," Russell replied.

"Thank you, Russell. You may leave now. Camerlengo, show him out," the Pope said calmly. "Also, send Ronnie and his team while you're at it."

The Camerlengo walked Russell out. He was shocked at what he had just witnessed. He knew that remote viewing was declassified, but he had no idea that it was still in practice, and that it could be so accurate. He gave in and popped another Xanax. Maybe he would treat himself to a Seroquel in a little bit. This entire thing was wrecking his nerves.

Chapter Twenty-Seven

"Hold up Jax, I just have to make a call real quick," I said and stopped at a pay phone. I hung up and we went through the boarding procedure. We finally ran into Rosette and Hannah.

"Oh my God! Baby, are you OK?" Hannah asked as she saw my face.

"I'll survive," I said.

"Damn, Newsdon, they got you good, eh?" Rosette said.

We sat down in first class. A little treat from the Jean fund. We talked about everything we'd been through and what could be the light at the end of the tunnel. None of us had any clue as to what Chile was going to bring us. Also, we hadn't completely decoded the letter from the old Pope. What other information might be buried in that letter? I would say one thing though. Jackson had saved my ass not once but twice so far, and I was grateful to have him in my life.

"Jackson, I just wanted to thank you for everything you've done for me so far. I literally can't do this without you," I said.

"Don't mention it, Graham. You, me, all of us here are quantumly entangled," he said, and flashed a smile.

God, even with everything going on, he's still a physics nerd. I flashed him a smile back.

The flight was a turbulent one. I once heard a physicist say that if he could ask God two questions they would be 'Why relativity' and 'why turbulence.' I think of that from time to time when I see Jackson. Hannah and Rosette were talking about the new Rising CD and I decided it was time to take a nap.

I woke up when we had to switch planes in Santiago. We had a short ride to our final destination, but no matter how you cut it, transferring planes sucks. We boarded the new flight and Jackson ordered himself a Captain and Coke, a drink that used to be one of my favorites. Rosette ordered herself a little bottle of wine. I was impressed with her; she didn't pop a Xanax and sexually harass us both this time. Maybe that was reserved for when she's with just us.

We finally landed in Antofagasta and rented a car. We drove to our hotel and set up shop.

"OK, it's hot as hell out right now and we're probably going to need to dig since it's all sand out there," I said. The two water jobs had been easy compared to the work we were going to have to put in on this one. "I'm going to find a shovel."

I took the car to a local store, where I bought two shovels and asked the owner for directions. The problem was that where we were going was literally in the middle of nowhere.

He told me to take Route 26 or Route 28, both connect to Route 5. The Mano can be found between mile markers 1309 and 1310. It is easy to reach from either direction and can be seen well in advance. If you're going to drive out for a visit, be sure you have sunscreen, plenty of water, and a full tank of gas. Take caution, driving in the seemingly endless salt flats can have a wearying effect and don't let the monotony trick you into driving too fast; too many fatal accidents have occurred in the desert, as evidenced from the dozens of skeletal wrecks and roadside shrines. I thanked him for his honesty and candor and returned to the hotel. Now all we had to do was wait for dark, when the desert wouldn't be so hot.

We watched TV for a little while and tried to decode the letter.

"Ouija lens and Drastic Ouijas. What do you suppose that means?" I asked a baffled room.

"Ouija boards work due to the ideomotor effect in psychology," Rosette offered.

"I'm not sure how that helps us figure out what we're supposed to do," said Hannah.

"We'll figure it out guys, it's not important right now," Jackson said.

"How do we know it's not important now?" I asked.

"Just trying to help, man," he said.

We went downstairs to the cafe for dinner. We sat and talked until the sun started to set.

"Alright guys, let's go," I said.

We piled into the car and started driving, following the store owner's directions. After about an hour and a half, we saw it out of the corner of our eyes. *This is it*, I thought, as my stomach started to tie itself in knots.

We pulled over to the side of the road and waited for the lone car about a quarter mile behind us to pass. When it finally did, we got out and grabbed our shovels.

"OK, so ten meters from the hand. So back it up thirty feet and start digging," Hannah said.

We dug our shovels into the fresh sand and dug for about forty minutes until finally I spoke up. "Guys, there's nothing here," I said, out of breath.

"It has to be. The first two were right where they were supposed to be, this third one must be here. What does the letter say?" Hannah said.

"Ten meters from the backwards day. Or night; go dig thirty feet at night," Rosette said.

We put our shovels down and looked around. We had about an eight-foot hole in front of us but no capstone. I started getting frustrated until Rosette squealed. I hope she has something good.

"I got it. OK, so you just dug ten meters from the hand, but it's not the hand. It's the backwards day. Or Yad. Day backwards is Yad. OK, so in Jewish culture the Yad is a pointer that you read the Old Testament with. It's a brass pointer finger," she said. "It is here. Jax, dig about five feet to the right."

Nobody else had any bright ideas, so we moved over five feet and started digging again. After about a half hour we heard a thud. Rosette squealed. "Boom, bitches," she said.

Jackson helped me load the chest out of the ground. It looked like the Ark of the Covenant. A chill went down my spine.

"I'll take that," an unfamiliar voice said. We spun around and saw three men standing behind us with guns drawn. "Oh good, you've already dug your graves for us. That was very kind and thoughtful of you. So, we don't have to. The box now," he said.

Jackson picked the box up over his head and walked over to where the men were standing and put it down.

"Let me introduce myself to you, since it's not going to matter in a little bit anyways. Formalities, you know, and mother always taught me to be polite. My name is Ronnie. And you kids have been a royal pain in the ass for almost a year now. We were just going to let you live and take your own life, Graham, but your friend has been a pesky motherfucker," he said, and backhanded Jackson with the gun. Rosette cried out. Ronnie pointed the gun at her next.

"Wait, don't!" Jackson screamed.

"So, like I was saying. We've been following you since you landed here. We didn't know what to make of you at first, but you are all really smart. Apparently too smart for your own good. Once I get this back to the Vatican, we'll have it destroyed like we should have done a long time ago. Doesn't matter if you have the other two," he said, as he cocked his gun. "You'll be dead, so at the end it doesn't really matter now does it? Alright, everybody walk."

He marched us down to the hand and had us get on our knees with our hands above our heads.

"Now which one should I get first?" he asked. "The muscle? The girlfriend? The wiseass girl? I want to make sure that you go last, friend," he said.

"Stop it!" Rosette yelled.

"Shut up," he said, and smacked her across the face.

"I'll kill you for this," Jackson said angrily as he rose to his feet and charged at Ronnie. Ronnie sidestepped him and tripped him right back into the sand.

"Young love. It's such a special thing, isn't it?" He sneered. "Now get back over there," he finished.

Jackson dusted himself off and walked back to us. Got on his knees, closed his eyes and started praying.

"Yes, I think I'll get rid of the muscle first. Thank you kindly for making this such an easy decision for me. Now all of you, close your eyes." Ronnie cocked his gun again.

Jackson closed his eyes, and we heard two gunshots. Rosette screamed. We opened our eyes expecting to see Jackson dead, but he was still there. We all were. In fact, two of the men Ronnie was with were dead on the ground. We heard another shot. This hit Ronnie in the leg. He dropped his gun. The wound was about an inch from his femoral artery. He would still have a tough time not bleeding out.

"What the hell just happened?" Hannah asked crying.

The phone call I made from the airport was to two Marines from my brother's battalion, Brayden and LJ. The same guys who had helped me out of the jam with the President. I couldn't risk another issue, and I knew they were good for it. I can't believe they got on a plane and made it to us that quickly. Another thirty seconds and Jackson would have been dead. They walked toward us out of the darkness.

"You guys OK?" Brayden asked.

"We are now. Where were you? Cutting it a little close there, guys," I said, still trying to catch my breath.

"We parked about a half mile down, in case someone was here they wouldn't see us," LJ said.

"Well, thank God you got here when you did," Hannah said.

We grabbed the chest. It was dark and I couldn't see anything written on it.

"Here, take our night vision goggles. They're in color," Brayden said.

"Seriously?" Jackson said.

"As a heart attack," LJ said.

"I still might have one of those," I said as we loaded the chest into the trunk. We started walking back to the car when we heard groaning.

"You bastard kids are never going to get away with this." Ronnie said.

I walked back to him and stuck my finger in his bullet wound. He screamed.

"What is so special about these fucking capstones that is worth dying for?" I asked.

Ronnie was still wincing from the pain, but a smile crept across his face. He started laughing hysterically. This was too much for Hannah, so we had to get out of there.

"We're going to go, guys," I said to Brayden and LJ.

"Don't worry about us, brother. We'll clean up. Looks like you guys did the hard work for us already,"

Brayden said as he pointed to the two holes in the ground and started laughing.

"What about Ronnie?" I asked.

"He'll never bother you or anyone else again, don't worry," LJ said.

We said our goodbyes and I told them that they had to come over and have dinner once this all cleared up. That was twice now they'd saved my life.

We got into the car, and I put on the goggles and looked at the box. It had writing clear as day above the lock. It was only padlocked. We could hammer it open when we got back to the hotel.

Alnitak, Alnilam and Mintaka must be in correct alignment to see the most Northern Lights

We spent the trip back to the hotel trying to figure out what that meant. On the way there, I had an epiphany.

"Let me see that letter again," I said to Rosette.

"Sure," she said. She had just barely stopped crying from before.

"I shook the sand off me and looked at the letter. "Drastic Ouijas and Ouija Lens," I said out loud. I took a pen out of the glove box and started marking the page up. These had to be anagrams.

"The Church frowns upon Ouija boards. They consider it summoning the devil," Rosette said.

"There's something here, I just can't see what it is," I said.

I played around with words as we drove. We brought the chest into the room and Jackson went downstairs to get a hammer. We knocked the lock off the chest and opened it up. There it was, the third capstone. Nothing more, nothing less. I was still sitting on the bed working things out with the letter when I finally figured it out.

"Drastic Ouijas is an anagram for Judas Iscariot," I said.

"It is not," Hannah said.

"To stop Judas Iscariot, you have to see through the Ouija Lens. Ouija Lens is an anagram for Jean-Louis."

"Who the hell is Jean-Louis?" Jackson asked.

I took a deep breath. "He's the Pope's Camerlengo," I said.

We sat there in silence for a few, then debated whether or not this was a suicide mission. The Vatican was already trying to kill us.

"This is the old Pope's dying wish. He wouldn't have put us through all of this if he didn't think it would help," I said as I whipped out my cell phone.

"What are you doing, baby?" Hannah asked.

I took another deep breath. "I'm emailing the Camerlengo," I said.

Chapter Twenty-Eight

The Camerlengo woke up in the morning thinking nothing was different. He showered, took a Xanax, made himself breakfast and sat down at his computer to see what was going on. He was surprised to see that he had received an email at two AM. He didn't think he knew anybody that would be up that late.

From: GrahamNewsdon@Protonmail.com

The Camerlengo's eyes grew wide and his heart skipped a beat. Was this really happening?

Hello Camerlengo. As you undoubtedly know by now, my name is Graham Newsdon. What I'm about to tell you is no secret, but I want to make my intentions well known.

It was early last year when my brother was killed on a mission to Syria which led us to a cryptogram from him which tied in the Bible, the Vatican and the Order of the Jesuits. Even the President of the United States got wrapped up in it. We survived that. I had thought that it was Pope Ignatius the First who had orchestrated everything, since he was the first Jesuit in office.

I have recently found out that he was a figurehead and not the person they wanted in power. As you may or may not have known, he was murdered. He was not the person we were after. That person is the new Pope, Aurora Toss I.

Pope Ignatius left us a bunch of clues to figure out what was going on. He destroyed evidence of the locations of the capstones for the Church. We have secured all three. He left a story imprinted on a vial of his DNA for us to find. Finally, he advised that in order to stop the madness that is happening in the Vatican, we should trust you and enlist your help. To be honest, I was skeptical at first, because I know you are the Pope's right-hand man, but I am taking a leap of faith.

We are set to reattach the capstones tomorrow evening. As you read this, we are already on our way to Cairo. The men that he sent after us in Chile are now dead. What I'm about to offer you is a onetime thing.

We know that reattaching the capstones will do something so powerful that it will bring established religion to its knees. We just have no idea what that is. If you know, now would be a good time to tell us.

I will be making my way to Rome after I reattach them, to confront Pope Aurora Toss I myself, I will need your help sneaking me in. If you have loyalty to your dead friend, I would like to think that you can be trusted.

I know that things have not been normal since he was killed, and everything is in disarray. If you would like to help, please reply to my email; it is encrypted and cannot be hacked. Nobody will be the wiser. I await your response. Thank you.

-Graham

The Camerlengo sat back and reflected on what he'd read until he heard a knock on the door.

"Everything OK, Camerlengo?" the Pope said.

The Camerlengo thought about that for a minute. Everything in him was telling him that he should tell the Pope what was happening, but his heart stopped him. Deep down he knew that Graham was right. Maybe it was time that faith was recalibrated. He just wished he knew what the capstones were going to do.

"Everything is fine, Your Holiness," the Camerlengo said as he closed his laptop.

"Good," the Pope said. He turned to leave, and then turned back. "You know something, Camerlengo? I really have to admire the work you've been doing here and everything you've done to help out with this situation. You're a man of faith, and that should never be questioned," the Pope said as he left.

That was unexpected. The Pope never had any kind words for him. He'd always been creepy and shady from the beginning. Jean-Louis decided that he was not going to be sucked in by this man in the white frock. He opened his computer back up and emailed Graham.

To GrahamNewsdon@Protonmail.com
Subject: OK

Hello Graham,

Yes, I've heard much about your travels and the difficulties you've been causing us since your brother died. Pope Ignatius was never a big fan of yours, but he hardly would have countenanced what this Pope has done against you. He was a man of faith, but he also knew that secrets cannot rest safe for eternity. I am aware of the vial of DNA, I took him to the doctor to have it extracted.

You are correct. My loyalty lies with him. I've been struggling with his death. I recently went to the apartment of a man here and found some poison in his garbage can. Although they cannot autopsy the Pope, I am convinced that he was murdered. This is the same man that first went to kill you, but your friend took his life instead.

The truth is that I am an old and tired man and sometimes things get so messed up that you have to burn it to the ground and let it rise out of its ashes like the Phoenix. I will help you, Graham. Just let me know when you are coming to Rome and I will have somebody escort you in. Please be advised though that if you do come in, you might not make it out alive. Keep in touch.

-Jean Louis

The Camerlengo sat back in his chair and took out a mini cigar from his cabinet. If this was the way this was all going to go down, he was not going to stand in anybody's way. He finished his cigar and took a Seroquel. He knew it would knock him out for a few hours, but it was better than being stuck inside his own mind. He had about an hour to set everything up.

When he awoke, the Camerlengo made his way to the College of Cardinals and pulled Cardinal Sorrentino aside.

"Camerlengo. This is most unusual of you to request such a direct meeting. Have you notified the Pope?" Sorrentino asked.

"I have not. I have come to speak to you directly, Cardinal," Jean-Louis replied.

"What can I help you with?" he asked.

"Perhaps it's best if we speak in my office."

They walked back to his office. On the way, they shared thoughts about God, life, and the wisdom that they had gathered in their 115 years of combined life experience. Finally, they reached Jean-Louis's office.

"What can I do for you, Camerlengo?" Cardinal Sorrentino asked again.

"It's about Graham Newsdon."

"What about him?"

The Camerlengo took a deep breath. This was the time to tell him everything. He was either going to run to the Pope with it, or he was going to be on board with it. He needed him on board as he was going to have to be the one to let him in.

"He reached out to me this morning," he said. He felt the Seroquel start to give his stomach the fuzzies.

"He did what?"

"Please, sit down and read," said the Camerlengo.

Cardinal Sorrentino sat down and the Camerlengo showed him his correspondence with Graham. Sorrentino read the whole thing and sat back in thought.

"Camerlengo," he said.

"Yes sir?"

"Do you have any of those cigars left?"

"But of course." The Camerlengo went into his cabinet and took one out, cut the tip off and lit it for the cardinal.

"You do realize this goes against everything we believe in?" asked Sorrentino.

"I do."

The Cardinal took a few puffs from the cigar. He let the smoke linger in his mouth for a little bit before he blew it out. He always enjoyed a good cigar during stressful times.

"Alright, Camerlengo, I must admit that I did admire the previous Pope and always found his death to be suspicious. I don't very much like our current one. I think he bullied his way in there by scaring everyone regarding this situation," he said, as he took a few more puffs of his cigar. He sat and thought for a few more minutes as only a wise man can. "If I am to come on board with you, I assume that nobody else can know," he said.

"That's correct. He's going to let me know when he's in Rome and we'll send a car out to get him. We'll say he's a diplomat. However, you're the one that's going to have to lead him in, I don't have that authority," Jean-Louis said.

"Interesting," said Sorrentino. "I will say this, though. There are many that are none too happy with this current Pope. They think that this has been a giant distraction from great Church matters. It would be a lot easier if I could gather a few," he said, as the Camerlengo cut him off.

"Nobody but you can know."

Sorrentino sat back and puffed his half-finished cigar. He stubbed it out and turned to the Camerlengo. "Alright, I'm in," he said.

The Camerlengo released a huge sigh of relief; he felt he could breathe again.

"Thank you, Cardinal. I appreciate your secrecy in this matter very much. Now I have some work to do. Everything must remain business as usual." The truth was, his Seroquel was starting to kick in and he was going to pass out in a few minutes.

"I will speak to you soon, Camerlengo. Thank you for trusting me," Sorrentino said as he left the room.

The Camerlengo shut the door behind him and locked it. Everyone knew when his door was locked, he was hard at work. He dusted off the reclining chair and sank down and closed his eyes. When he woke up, he should have another email from Graham.

Chapter Twenty-Nine

We boarded the first flight to Cairo that we could after I sent the Camerlengo that email. By the time we got on the plane, I had already received his response saying he was in. I had to plan this extremely carefully, as I was going to be going alone. I wasn't going to have Jackson with me. Once again, Rosette popped a Xanax and ordered herself a drink. I couldn't fault her, not after what we'd been through. What she and Jackson had been through. She acted tough, but deep down she was the sensitive type. My girlfriend, however, was passed out, no medication required. I was just hoping Rosette wasn't about to have a few drinks and strip for Jackson, knowing how she got.

I wanted to see what was on the in-flight TV. I caught Jackson's eye and we gave each other a heads up. Wouldn't you know it, Blur was going international. I found him on the last channel. He seemed to be in the middle of a diatribe about how the music industry was run by devil worshipping global elitists. I turned it off. I have a very love-hate relationship with that guy. Sometimes I feel like he's right on the money, and other times I'm mortified by what comes out of his mouth. I wasn't even about to start searching the internet for devil worship in the entertainment industry. Jackson was still awake, so I turned to him.

"Hey Jax," I said.

"Yeah bro?"

"Did you know that the Ten Commandments were lifted from the Egyptian Book of the Dead, Chapter 125?" I asked.

"No, I did not know that. Is that right?"

"That's right. Also, the word Amen comes from Amun-Ra one of the Gods of the Egyptian culture. When you say Amen in Church, you are actually giving praise to Amun-Ra."

"Very interesting," he said.

"It is. In fact, much of our everyday spiritual life can be traced back to the Egyptians," I said.

"Well, that's interesting. But did you know that some infinities are larger than others?" he asked.

I couldn't wrap my mind around that. He chuckled to himself while I struggled with that concept.

"Here's an even better one. Did you know that the conscious observer collapses the waveform into a singularity, but before observation things can exist in simultaneous superpositions? We've been able to verify a particle that's been up to seven places at the same time until observed," he said.

I was beginning to feel sorry that I'd ever begun this conversation with him. With all this seemingly voodoo stuff going on, how can we numb down an almighty being that created everything known and unknown into what three books have dumbed him down to be? Shit, I was beginning to sound like Jackson. I was going to bring up the fact that well before the Church acknowledged the Copernicus model, Julian the Apostate, who was Constantine's nephew, described the planets revolving around the Sun more than a millennia earlier. In fact, I'm probably going to butcher this, but I believe he said something like 'The Sun is the fiery chariot that all the planets dance around,' but I didn't want him to blow my mind again. I did, however, share with him the conclusion I had. In Jean's letter it said it all begins with Christ the Redeemer, but that statue had nothing to do with our adventure. It was the symbolic Hands out, the Hands of God or should I say the hands reaching to God that we had found. Just then Rosette turned around.

"Hey, Newsdon. Why are you wearing sandals?" she asked. I could smell the drinks on her breath.

"Because they're comfortable," I replied.

"Don't you know we've been pretty much running for our lives the last two weeks? Your feet look like two bags of chopped meat," she said.

"Honey, be nice." Jackson laughed, which caused her to laugh.

"You really should use that Ped Egg thing for dry skin. Although I feel like if you use it the right way you'd be as tall as your girlfriend afterwards." She and Jackson laughed again.

"Alright, fine, I'll put shoes on." I opened my carryon and threw on some boat shoes.

"Hey Jax, do you know how to say peace be unto you in Hebrew and in Arabic?" I asked.

"Since when do you speak Jewish?" Rosette asked, still a little buzzed.

"In Arabic it's As-Salaam Alaykum. In Hebrew it's Shalom Aleichem. Don't you think that's pretty fucking close to one another? Why can't they just realize they are brothers?" I asked.

"I don't have a good answer for you, brother man, but I do see your point," Jackson said.

For the next hour or so I watched David Wilcock on Gaia TV. One of my cousins sent me a link a while back, and I got hooked on it. Eventually my eyes started to feel heavy, and I put my chair back and went to sleep.

I woke up as we were landing in Cairo. The plan was to rent a car and go directly to the hotel. The only problem was that the hotel was rather far from the Pyramids, and during the daytime they are a tourist trap. We were going to have to wait a few hours to go out at night. In the hotel, we unzipped the large duffel bag that had the three capstones in it. We took a look at them together and I noticed that, since we had arrived in Egypt, they seemed to be a little warmer to the touch. They also seemed to be vibrating at a very low frequency. They must have known they were close to their rightful location. All at once I was overwhelmed thinking about how many generations and centuries this secret has been kept from the world. This was immediately followed with the unrealistic yet plausible reality that when we put them up, it might just destroy the planet. But that was just the optimist in me.

Just then I noticed that there were etchings on the back of all three. They were the names of the three stars on Orion's Belt. They must have to be placed on the correct pyramid directly under them. I shared this with the others, and they looked relieved. That's what that statement was about before. I didn't think any of us wanted to climb a pyramid with this and have to climb back down and go back up again.

We waited until it got dark then got in our car with all our gear, including the color night vision goggles we'd gotten from Brayden and LJ. We only had two pairs, though. Jackson volunteered to go up dark. Rosette was going to climb the smallest pyramid, as she was more athletic than Hannah.

It took us about fifteen minutes to get there, and we pulled over to the side of the road and divided up the capstones, making sure each one went under the correct star. I took a deep breath and turned to Hannah.

"You know I love you, babe," I said.

"I know, I love you too," she said.

"No, like, I need you to know. If something happens here now, or if something happens in Rome after this, I'd never forgive myself." I took a deep breath and dropped to one knee. "Hannah Husker, will you be my Hannah Newsdon?" I took out the ring she always wanted: heart-shaped with a diamond in the middle.

She started to cry but quickly cleaned herself up and said yes! We celebrated for a few minutes as Rosette teased Jackson. I put the ring on her finger. I had been planning to do this for a while now, but life had gotten in the way.

"Alright, you two. Come on, we've got work to do." Rosette took a deep breath and started marching towards her pyramid.

"Congrats, brother. Didn't think you had it in you." Jackson started walking towards the biggest pyramid.

"Love you baby, I'll be back." I said to Hannah.

"I love you so much," she said.

"Wait, I almost forgot." I handed her my phone with the extension zoom on it. "Whatever happens, whatever you see, just film it," I said.

"You got it, love bug," she said, and went back to the car and sat on the hood.

I was halfway up my pyramid, sweating my you-know-what off, and the others were already at the top. From what I could see, it looked like they had put the capstones on already. I didn't want to scream, partially because they wouldn't hear me. I wished I had splurged for some walkie-talkies.

I finally made it to the top and looked around. It was very unassuming, but there seemed to be some kind of conducting wire sticking up. *Guess this is where I put the capstone on. OK, here goes nothing.*

The second—and I mean the second—I put the third capstone in place, it started vibrating more strongly, and got warmer to the touch. All at once, a bright flash of light came down from the sky, as thin as headphone wire, directly into the top of the capstone. It vibrated some more. Next the entire pyramid shook, and I nearly fell off, catching myself at the last minute. After the pyramid shook, the capstone itself which was black as onyx turned white like the light that had come down. It seemed to have a pulsating rhythm to it. I looked at the other two pyramids and Jackson and Rosette were already halfway down, but theirs were doing the same thing. In fact, they were pulsating in unison. I stood up there mesmerized. They would pulsate bright white almost like a club light and then a flash of light would come down a moment later. I decided it was time to climb down, as I didn't want to be killed by another tremor.

I climbed down the pyramid slowly but surely. I saw Hannah in the distance still vigilantly filming this entire ordeal. *She must have half an hour of footage by now*, I thought. I saw Rosette and Jackson holding each other by Hannah as well. It took me about ten minutes to rejoin them. I turned around to look at what was going on.

The lights that went into the capstone were brilliant. I watched the display for a few minutes, and it looked like the light went into the capstones and it charged them, then the capstones would blink in patterns for a few then stop. Then another light would hit them, and the cycle would start again. I looked into the distance and saw a swarm of cars coming in our direction.

"Alright guys, I think it's time to take our leave," I said.

"Good idea," Jackson said.

We got in the car and were about to take off, but Hannah was still filming. I got out and called to her. "Baby we have to go now!" I said.

"Hold on, just a few more minutes," she said.

I ran to her and picked her up and carried her to the car and put her in the backseat with Rosette. She was not too happy about it. We sped off towards our hotel.

We got to the hotel and turned on the news. Although we didn't understand the language, there was a reporter on site talking about the lights. Nobody seemed to know what was going on and everybody around seemed a little freaked out. There were also Praise be Allah signs all over the place as they believed this was a divine act. I honestly had no idea what it meant.

We connected the phone to the TV, hoping to find some clues. Just as I had thought, the moment I placed the capstone on the pyramid it started acting up. We watched the entire hour and ten minutes of video that Hannah had taken, but nothing leaped out at us. We started over, and, after fifteen minutes, Rosette had an idea.

"Look. You see three short bursts and then one long burst and then three short bursts. This pattern repeats itself," she said.

What could it be? Communication? Code? Instructions? Was it in a language? Where was this light coming from?

"Jackson, you have any ideas, man?" I asked.

"Just one, but I'm not sure yet, it's probably nothing," he said.

We watched for another fifteen minutes and noticed that other patterns were forming. I grabbed a piece of paper and started writing them all down. Three short, one long, three short. Two short, one long. One short four long. Three short three, long three short. I stopped writing.

"Rewind that back to 30:56," I said.

Hannah rewound it, and we saw three short bursts three long bursts, and then three short bursts.

"Again," I said.

Again she rewound.

Three short, three long, three short.

A chill went up my spine.

"Guys, do you recognize that pattern?" I asked.

"No," they said in unison.

"That's Morse code for SOS," I said. "What if this entire thing is Morse code?"

"This light looks like it's coming directly from the three stars on Orion's Belt. How would it be Morse Code if it's not from here? Assuming it was someone sending a signal, how would they know about Morse Code? And how would they know English?" Hannah asked. She did have a point.

"Start this video over from the beginning." I pulled out a few pieces of paper and a pen. I looked up the Morse Code chart on my phone and started playing the video, pausing, writing things down, checking it against the list on my phone.

This proved to be an incredibly tedious task. We slowed it down a bunch of times and kept the timestamp visible on the video so we always knew exactly where we were. To do fifteen minutes' worth of video took me an hour and a half. I had to take a break.

We took a break to get soda from the vending machine down the hall. This particular hotel didn't serve any alcohol. My hands were getting tired from transcribing, but this was something that had to be done.

We went back into the room, and I took over again. I got a second wind and continued on decoding this message. This time it went by a little easier. I got the next twenty minutes done in an hour.

We took another break, this time to go outside and have a cigarette. Well, I had a cigarette, the other three were just staring at the lights flashing in the distance. By this point we could see a giant crowd was forming by the pyramids. We went back in and I grabbed another Fanta—unfortunately, that was all they had. Then we sat back down.

"Can you read it to us, please?" Hannah asked.

"Not yet, I want to hear it when it's done," Rosette said.

"I agree with Rose, guys. Let's just wait for it to be done and then we can figure out what we're going to do," Jackson said.

"Agreed," I said.

I continued to translate through the night. This was very tricky because missing one letter or word might change the entire message. We had no idea what we were about to read.

I ended up finishing the translation at around four in the morning. It had taken me about two and a half hours to finish up the last forty-five minutes, as I was getting tired.

"OK, guys. Are you ready, or should we do this in the morning?" I asked.

"Let's do it in the morning. I am exhausted," Rosette said.

"Yeah, sleep with the papers, don't lose them." Jackson and Rosette went into their bedroom.

I got about eight hours of sleep and woke up around one PM. There was a loud noise coming from outside and when we looked out the window, we saw a massive crowd by the pyramids taking pictures. Some were praying, some were crying. It was hard to tell from our vantage point exactly what we were seeing. I knocked on the door to Jackson and Rosette's room.

"OK guys, are you ready for this?" I asked.

Truth be told, I barely remembered what I had translated last night. I was in a state of physical and mental exhaustion from climbing the pyramid and then focusing on the translation all night. "Here goes," I said.

Greetings family of light. Please forgive our rather archaic method of communication. Many of you are still not ready to receive such a blunt message as a visit. We can't tell you how happy we are that you have reconnected our method of communication that you had disconnected such a long time ago. Oh joyous day.

You are probably wondering how we speak your language, and how this message came to you so quickly when we are 445 light years as you call it away. We'll get to that.

We are what you call the Plaedians. We are the seven sisters. Our closest star would be known as Electra to you. We have watched you evolve since we gave you guidance many thousands of years ago. We are sad to say that the state of your planet and the people on it give us worry.

We have traveled the cosmos. Some of the things that we have learned to do, or what will happen to us, will be too strong for you to comprehend at your current state of evolution. This is not meant to worry you, only to inspire you to strive for greater things. When the time comes, we will guide you.

We are able to monitor you by sending our consciousness down to your planet to observe. As you are starting to figure out now, particles as you call them can be in multiple places at the same time. This is just a manipulation of the soul or the ethos. This is how we know of your planet's language of English.

We have learned to manipulate the energy of the stars for everything we need. To nourish ourselves, for fuel, for energy. You are still relying on aged ways of energy creation such as nuclear power, gasoline, and oil. These will fade out eventually. Knowledge always moves forward.

As one of your greats on your planet was able to figure out, moving at the speed of light is impossible because what you call the mass of the object would hit infinite mass as it approaches that speed. What you don't know is that you can manipulate particles that already go faster than the speed of light to carry material with pinpoint accuracy. You call them Tachyons and right now they are merely hypothetical to you. What you don't know is that the energy it takes decreases once you're faster than the speed of light. The faster it moves, the less energy it requires. That is how we are able to manipulate so precisely. That is also how we were able to send a message down from what you call the stars of Orion's Belt, directly into the pyramids. We are cosmically not far from Orion's Belt and this technology has been available to us for what you would consider an incredibly long time.

We are not here to scare you or interfere. In fact, a long time ago Earth was considered a free will zone, and its beings would have dominion over your planet as they saw fit. Sadly, this is not going as well as we had hoped. War and violence has been rampant since the dawn of your collective uplifted consciousness into sentient beings.

Throughout your galaxy alone, there are millions of planets with life on them. You just don't have the tools yet to observe them. Also, the way you search for life is by searching for compounds such as water and oxygen and carbon-based elements. How you came to be. This is not how the Great Designer created everywhere. When your scientists start thinking outside the box, as you say, they will be able to find life.

We have sent you this message as a short reintroduction to let you know that you are not alone. Quite honestly, we are a little surprised, with your knowledge of the vastness of this observable universe, never mind the multiverse, that many of you still think you are all alone. We are here to reassure you that you are not, and that once people learn to be kind to one another and live in harmony with each other, we will make further contact. Please note that every time you make a religion out of something, it always loses the essence of what it was supposed to convey to begin with. Which is love. Prime Creator is love unbounded. Why do you exist? Because you have to. Nothing is an accident. With much love and peace, we will talk at a later time as you call it.

We all sat there for a few minutes, thinking about what I had just read. It was a lot to take in. Could this be real? I had to get some answers.

"Jax?" I asked.

"Yeah, man," he replied.

"From a physics standpoint, is what this message talking about possible?"

He sat silently rereading the passage. I don't think I've ever seen his brain working so hard in my life. Finally, he spoke up.

"In April 2010, radio astronomers that had been working at the Jodrell Bank Observatory saw an unknown object in galaxy M82 that was sending radio signals. This had never been seen before and the object was moving four times the speed of light. In a hypothetical sense, it sounds crazy, but it just might be possible. The only thing is that it would lead to a violation of causality and completely destroy every known law of physics. But Tachyons are hypothetical particles that hypothetically will do just that. Go faster than the speed of light. Also, it is possible that particles can react in a hyper state or multiple locations at once. Is this possible? I mean who the hell knows. The message was clear as day from your decoding of it and it could be possible. Hell, we don't even know what dark matter is yet, so I have no idea."

I remembered the crystal that my brother had embedded information into. An article about pulling the oxygen and hydrogen molecules apart and using hydrogen as energy with only the Sun to do the work came to mind. Maybe we were just in a place right now where we had to make a leap of faith. There are things that we just don't understand. My mind quickly shifted to a story I heard about of someone named Pam Reynolds.

Pam Reynolds was a singer-songwriter who had a tumor at the base of her brain stem. She wasn't given much time to live; however, the doctors came up with a radical idea for surgery. They would chill her body temperature down to 60 degrees, drain the blood from her head, remove the tumor, send the blood back in and gradually warm her back up. Her eyes were taped shut completely and her ears had plugs in them that made clicking noises. The clicking noises would register brain stem activity as they could only begin the procedure when her brain stem stopped reacting to it. If they had started it earlier, she would have bled out. So, both her eyes and ears were blocked, and she was clinically dead.

From there she was pulled out of her body and floated above it and in the room. She felt more aware, more conscious than being alive felt. She was able to identify the instrument used to cut her open, and she heard conversations between the staff working on her, despite the constant clicking noises in her ears. She then felt she was pulled towards a light and made out deceased relatives.

When she awoke, she relayed this information to the doctors, making very specific mentions of what had happened while she was out that basically scared the shit out of them. The difference between this near-death experience and other people's was that this one was medically monitored and nobody had any idea of how it could be possible that she would retain new information after her body was dead.

I told this story to everyone as this was the moment I began to believe in the afterlife and in God. There was so much that we didn't know, but what I did know was what we thought we knew, was vastly incomplete. I started to think that maybe it was possible we had really received this message and that it was true. All at once Rosette stopped us.

"Hey guys, you need to listen to this message I just found," she began. "It's a message from the Plaedians that was made through a channeler called Abraham. It had been on AquaStream for a few years now," she said, playing it for us.

"There are multitudes of cultures and societies that exist throughout the vastness of space, and these societies and cultures have been on and off this planet from the very beginning.

"It is not just that we, the Pleiadians, have come to assist. We are only one grouping, from one star system. There are many who have journeyed here for many reasons. The majority of the extra-terrestrials are here for your uplift, though there are also those who are here for other reasons.

"We give our version of things, only to bring you into higher consciousness. We do not wish to say that this version, and only this version is how it is. This whole teaching is designed with the great purpose in mind, and the stories that we tell you are set up to take you to a higher plane of consciousness. That is our intention.

"You are magnificent beings, members of the Family of Light, and you come to Earth at this time on an

assignment to create a shift, to make a change, to assist in the transition.

"You were told before you came here that there would be much assistance, and that at different junctures of your development, different entities would present themselves upon the planet in different capacities, to trigger you, to fire you up, to remind you, but not to do it for you. We are one of those triggers, a catalyst. When you hear the name Pleiadians you feel a connection, because we are assisting you in bringing your own information, your own knowing, forward.

"You yourself chose to be here. You are on assignment to bring memory forward, and to bring the value of human existence, back to the forefront of Creation. You are needed. You have been in training for this assignment for lifetimes. You did not come unprepared. All that you need to know now is inside of you, and it is your task to remember your training. This is not a lifetime when you are going to be taught new information.

"As we said before, this is the lifetime when you are going to remember what you already know, and we are just here to remind you of it. That is part of our assignment.

"Humanity is an experiment. Humanity has been designed, as has just about everything else that exists within Creation. Prime Creator began experimenting

with Creation a long time ago in this universe for the purpose of greater self-exploration, self-gratification, and self-expression. Prime Creator brought energies and essences of life, extensions of itself, into this universe, and endowed those extensions with the gifts that it had. Prime Creator said to these extensions of itself, 'Go out and create, and bring all things back to me.'

"Earth was a beautiful place, located on the fringes of one of the galactic systems, and easily reached from other galaxies. It was close to many 'way portals', the highways that exist for energies to travel throughout space. Some of the creator gods were master geneticists. They designed various species, some human, some animal, by playing with the varieties of DNA, that the sentient civilizations contributed to make Earth into an exchange center for information, a Light center, a living library. The original planners of Earth were members of the 'Family of Light', beings who worked for, and were associated with, an aspect of consciousness called Light.

"They designed a place where galaxies would contribute their information, and where all would be able to participate, and share their specific knowledge. Earth was to be a Cosmic Library, a place of incredible beauty that experimented with how information could be stored through frequencies, and through the genetic process.

"The project of the Living Library on Earth was eventually fought over. During Earth's early history, there were wars in space for ownership of this planet. Skirmishes took place, and Earth became a place of 'duality'. Certain creator gods who had the right to do whatever they wanted, because Earth is a 'free will zone', came in and took over. When the battles occurred, a certain group of entities fought in space, and won the territory of Earth.

"These new owners did not want the native Earth species, the humans, to be informed of what took place. Uninformed, the species would be easier to control. That is why Light is information, and darkness is lack of information. These entities beat out Light, and Earth became their territory.

"These new owners who came here three hundred thousand years ago, are the magnificent beings spoken of in your Bible, in the Babylonian and Sumerian tablets, and in texts all over the world.

"They came to Earth and rearranged the native human species. They rearranged your DNA in order to have you broadcast within a certain limited frequency band. These frequencies could feed them and keep them in power.

"The original human was a magnificent being, whose twelve strands of DNA were contributed by a

221

variety of sentient civilizations. When the new owners came in, they worked in their laboratories and created versions of humans with the two-stranded double helix DNA. The original pattern was left within the human cells, but it was not functional. It was split apart, un-plugged. We, as Pleiadians, came back through time, into what would perhaps be called our past. We came back in order to share a frequency with you, a frequency which each one of you has agreed to carry on this planet in order to change the DNA of the rearranged human race.

"Earth is assisting, in its own way, the evolution of the universe. It is where the plan begins to blossom, and what happens on Earth is going to affect many, many worlds.

"The creator gods who have been ruling this planet have the ability to become physical, though mostly they exist in other dimensions. They keep Earth in a certain vibrational frequency, while they create emotional trauma to nourish themselves. There are some beings who honor life before anything else. And there are also beings who do not honor life, do not understand their connection to it.

"Who are these beings who came in and rent asunder the original plans for Earth? Who are these space beings who are sometimes referred to as the Darteshas? These

space beings are part human and part reptilian. We call them the Lizzies, because we like to make things a little less emotional, a little humorous, so that you don't take them so seriously and get upset. We are not here to frighten you. We are here to inform you. They have fed off your emotions. One of the big secrets that has been kept from you as a species is the richness and wealth that accompanies emotion. You have been steered away from exploring emotion, because through emotion, you can figure things out. Your emotions connect you with the spiritual body. The spiritual body, of course, is non-physical, existing on a multi-dimensional sphere.

"Why are we telling you all this? Why do you need to know it? You need to know it because the Lizzie reality is reentering and merging with your dimension.

"As you awaken to your history, you will begin to open your ancient eyes. These are the eyes of Horace, which see not through the eyes of a human being, but from the point of view of a god. They see the connected-ness and purpose of all things. For the ancient eyes are able to see into many realities, and to connect the whole picture, the whole history.

"All of this is to be felt. Allow your brain cells to click into being without your rational conscious mind wanting to define things down to the most minute detail. This ex-perience involves raising a feeling inside yourself. And

then, one day, at one moment, in one afternoon, having an overwhelming sense of knowing, having a composition of a thousand pages long, come alive in five seconds of divine ecstasy.

"You hold the history of the universe within your physical body. What is occurring upon the planet now is the literal mutation of your physical body, for you are allowing it to be evolved to a point where it will be a computer that can house this information.

"Before you came into the body, all of you committed to designing events that would fire your codings or blueprints that would activate your memories. Then you came into the body, and you forgot. All of you have had your blueprints and codings fired to some extent because you understand that there is a divine purpose, or divine plan, that you are a part of.

"The firing of the codings and the realization of your identity are going to become phenomenally intense. The reason for this is the evolving DNA. When you have twelve helixes of DNA in place, those helixes will begin to plug into the twelve chakra system. The twelve chakras are vortex centers, loaded with information, that you must be able to translate.

"You have to become super-beings in whatever reality you enter, because as members of the Family of Light, the branch of renegades, this is your forte.

"As members of the Family of Light, you know the inside scoop. You come as ambassadors to make realities merge and become more informed within themselves, so that everyone involved can release fear and become uninhibited.

"As you grow, and come to these higher realms of recognition, you will break through layers of yourself that have held you down. Think of the frequency that has limited the human experiment as a radio station. The human experiment has had one radio station on for three hundred thousand years – same old tunes. The human experiment was unable to turn the dial and hear a different band. So, the same frequency was broadcast. This created a quarantine, a sealing off of this planet.

"The creative cosmic rays sent by Prime Creator and the original planners pierced through this frequency shield. They bombard Earth. However, they must have someone to receive them. Without a receptacle, these creative cosmic rays would create chaos and confusion. You, as members of the Family of Light, come into the system to receive these rays of knowledge. You then disseminate the knowledge, the new lifestyle, and the new frequency, to the rest of the population to alter the entire planet.

"The ultimate tyranny in this society is not control by martial law. It is control by the psychological

manipulation of consciousness, through which reality is defined, so that those who exist within it do not even realize that they are in prison. They do not even realize that there is something outside of where they exist. We represent what is outside of what you have been taught exists. It is where you sometimes venture, and where we want you to dwell. It is outside of where your society has told you, you can live.

"What we want more than anything else, is to assist you, as members of the Family of Light, to succeed in liberating the humans. Focus on the dance of yourself. To what tune will you dance, and to what magic will you perform, and to what heights will you be willing to push consciousness, to give it a new definition of possibilities?

"Members of the Bringers of the Dawn, or Family of Light, work in teams. You don't go into systems alone. You need each other to do this work, because you cannot hold the frequency by yourself. By going in as teams, you increase the odds of successfully carrying out the plan. You are like rays, and Light spirals of the central Sun that are very intelligent, and you are guided by a great intelligence inside the central Sun.

"The members of the Family of Light are much more than human. Characteristically, you are supreme achievers in the multi-dimensional realm. One applies for a position in the multi-dimensional realm as a

226

member of the Family of Light. If you were to have a business card printed up for yourself, when you are in full memory of your identity, it would say something like:

"'Renegade member of Family of light, system buster. Available for altering systems of consciousness within the Free Will Universe. On call'.

"We speak to you as if you are not human, because to us you are not. To us, you are members of the Family of Light. We know your multi-dimensional selves. We speak to you about dealing with humans, because it is your assignment to integrate with them, soothe them, and awaken a spark of Light within them, so they are all not destroyed, and so this place can house a new species, in a new realm of activity.

"Our final words include a thank you to all of you who recognize the Light Source that is a part of your identity, and that moves you to follow the silent whisperers that echo down the golden spirals, through the corridors of your own Being. We honor you. We recognize you. We are here to assist you. We are all here as the Family of Light, to bring that choice and that freedom to evolve back onto this planet. Family of light, wake up!"

The video finished and we sat looking at each other. Many of the idioms and phrases were similar, such as Prime Creator and free will zone. Is it possible that they had tried to communicate with us in different ways such as consciousness channeling?

"Guys, you know what I have to do again, right?" I asked.

"I was waiting for you to bring it up. Let's set up the lighting and I'll film it," said Jackson.

I was going to catch everyone up on AquaStream with another video. At this point if I died, I wanted to know that my life's work and knowledge was out in the open for people to find if they were interested. I also emailed the Camerlengo, telling him that I would be coming tomorrow and to have everything ready.

"Hello, everyone. I have a story to continue with you all. I hope you didn't miss me too much. So, what has happened since our last communication . . ." I began.

Chapter Thirty

The Camerlengo awoke in the morning to another email from Graham. He sat up, cracked his back; it was part of getting old. He then read Graham's message.

Dear Camerlengo (Jean-Louis),

I will be making my way to Rome first thing in the morning. By the time you wake up, I should be there. Sorry I couldn't tell you when I was coming or which flight. I rented a private jet to make this trip. I hope you understand.

I know everything. I mean everything. I know the secret that the Vatican has covered up, and I know what the Pope was so afraid to have leak out. I'm completely convinced that the old Pope Ignatius I, although we had issues in the past, was murdered due to his soft approach to me and my friends. However, he left us clues along the way that led us directly to you and to the story of the beginning of one of the world's greatest religions, until it became too big to control.

Ignatius hid information that we were able to decode. It seems that he knew something was going to happen to him and made sure to scramble this

information. I guess he didn't trust that the new Papacy would do right by the people of the world. This is information that they all should know about. If anarchy begins, it will eventually settle down and a new consciousness rising can begin. We can finally begin to appreciate God in a higher state of elevated thinking than the one that plagues this world.

Pope Aurora has sent multiple people after me, and I've almost lost my life a few times. I'm well aware that there is a chance I might not come out of this alive, but what I must do must be done. I will explain everything in further detail when I arrive. However, for now please see the following attachments.

The first is a document that shows how early Catholicism created Islam as a way to get Jerusalem back from the Jews. However, it multiplied like a virus until it was too late to do anything about. This entire document was embedded in a vial of Pope Ignatius I's DNA, and on a specific chromosome, and hidden away next to one of the capstones. I can't tell you how difficult it was to figure this one out.

The next attachment is a video which shows what happened in Egypt when we returned the capstones to their rightful places. Watch the entire video. Long story short, this was a message to us, sent in Morse Code.

The next attachment is a transcript of the decoded message. As you will see, this is why the Pope has been so active in chasing us. Please take your time with this and see to it that you let who needs to know, know before I get there.

I thank you for all your support during this. At one point I was a drunken medical student just trying to get through life. Then my brother was murdered. I never asked for this. I never asked to know everything that I know now, but you can be damn sure I'm going to finish it. See you soon.

-Graham

The Camerlengo read the first letter and his eyes bugged out of his head. He popped two Xanax. He felt frozen, in a cold sweat, trapped in his own body. But he knew the significance of what was about to happen, and he continued on and watched the video. Just a bunch of flashing lights. Yes, it made his heart jump into his throat, but it wasn't so bad. It was only when he read what was decoded that he slumped in his chair. All at once it hit him that the cardinals had no idea about any of this. They were kept in a hierarchy that provided them very little solace. It was comforting to the Camerlengo that at least by appearance, they were not alone in the

Universe. He took a sip of seltzer, closed his laptop and put it in his bag. He was going to see Cardinal Sorrentino.

The Camerlengo made his way to Cardinal Sorrentino's quarters. He caught him as he was leaving to go to the church to meet up with the other cardinals and the Pope. He wasn't sure what they would be discussing. Jean-Louis cornered Sorrentino and told him that they had to go inside before anybody saw them. He then told him that Graham had reached out to him and he would be arriving shortly. Jean-Louis turned on his computer so that Sorrentino could read the letter, then go through the attachments. After about thirty minutes, Cardinal Sorrentino spoke up.

"This is greater than anything I could have ever dreamed," he said. He was not prone to anxiety like the Camerlengo, but the moment overwhelmed him. Jean-Louis had a cigar that Cardinal Sorrentino enjoyed. He lit it for him.

"Thank you, Camerlengo," Sorrentino said. "Well, clearly something has to be done."

"I agree, Cardinal, but what exactly can we do?"

Just then an alert went off. He had a new email from Graham.

I am in St Peters Square right now. I am in an Italian Jersey with a plain black hat on. I am leaning on the Obelisk. I will wait here for twenty minutes. If I don't see someone coming to get me, I will disappear forever.

-Graham

Twenty minutes was not a lot of time. Sorrentino told the Camerlengo to make sure the cardinals were all gathered at the church and to tell the Pope that he was running late because of food poisoning. The Camerlengo left and Sorrentino changed into his street clothes, looking unassuming. He knew he had to get Graham into the Vatican, but how?

Chapter Thirty-One

I waited at the Obelisk in the boiling heat with a timer on my phone. I was not kidding. If I even sensed something was off, I was going to fly back, no questions asked, and let them sort the mess out between them. I checked my video and it had 800,000 hits so far. Not bad for less than twelve hours ago. It would continue to grow, and then there would be a mutiny. The government would try and paint me as a lunatic, much like they did with Alberto Rivera online. One thing was for sure though, I did have an endgame if things went sour here. After eighteen minutes and thirty seconds, a frail man approached me.

"You're Graham Newsdon? Of course you are, I recognize you from the videos. My name is Cardinal Sorrentino. The Camerlengo has told me all about what was going on here. Firstly, I must say how shocked I am that we have hidden information from the public for generations, centuries even. It's still a little hard to believe that it's all true, but I'm going on a leap of faith. What's your game plan?" he said.

"Take me in as your grandson, show me around and introduce me to the Pope. I've brought these." I said as I took out a fat stack of printed copies of Alberto's message and a stack of printed-out messages from the capstones. I was going to distribute these to the cardinals and hopefully they would confront the Pope about it.

We walked through the square and past the Swiss Guard, along a path within the immaculately kept Vatican grounds as I tried to take in everything. It's not that I was starstruck by the place, I just knew I would never come back in my lifetime, so I was trying to take it all in. After a few minutes of walking, the cardinal turned to me. "Wait right here," he said, and left me in the shade on a bench. I sat down, pulled my new hat brim down, put my sunglasses on and tried to look unassuming. I didn't want to be recognized until it was showtime.

I waited for a few minutes until I saw the cardinal coming back with another gentleman. I saw him pop a pill and dry swallow it. His hands were shaking. This must be the Camerlengo.

"Hello Graham, it's nice to finally meet you," the Camerlengo said.

"Likewise. Pope Ignatius had a lot of faith in you, so I reached out to you, simple as that. How soon can we get this started?" I asked.

"Mass ends in twenty minutes. After that we will go into the church."

"Great," I said.

We sat on the bench and talked about what we had each been up to. I told them when I realized something was wrong and was being covered up, and the Camerlengo advised the same thing. He told me that he found ricin in Silvio's apartment garbage and, knowing the Pope could not have an autopsy, started suspecting things then and there. Cardinal Sorrentino advised us that it was when the Pope started putting everything in front of his duties regarding this, that he sensed he was a little too close. They had told me that Pope Ignatius was originally not going to do anything about us. He never thought we'd get this far and didn't even know if any of what was supposedly out there was even real. He had about half the support of the Cardinals. The other half agreed with the head of the Jesuits at the time, the Black Pope, Aurelio. Then he mysteriously died like Pope John Paul I, and the new Pope, who was not even a cardinal, was ushered in. It was highly unorthodox how it all played out and the people didn't even know how to take that.

But once everything became about stopping me and my friends, people took fierce sides. The sad thing was most of them didn't know about the secrets they were putting lives at risk over. Now, although I knew most of this already, it was good to get confirmation that that was what had happened. The truth is, there was so much to be excited about in the future if this came out. Humanity had been stuck in a loop of low evolution. This would be the biggest secret to ever come out. Granted, I had already made a video about everything we'd been through, but videos were debatable. It really makes you wonder what Tom Delonge and To the Stars Academy of Arts and Sciences really know. Also, I had a plan.

The doors to the church opened and the cardinals started to shuffle their way out. At once, Cardinal Sorrentino stopped them and ushered them back inside. Many of them were confused as to what was happening, but they came back in and got back in their seats.

"Ah, Camerlego and Cardinal Sorrentino. So sorry you missed Mass this morning. It was a good one. We were talking about loyalty to God within the Church. Who's your friend?" the Pope asked.

"Pope Aurora Toss, I'd like you to meet Graham Newsdon," the Camerlengo replied.

The room went silent and then the Cardinals started murmuring amongst themselves. The Pope was in complete disbelief.

"Very funny, Camerlengo, no really, who is this?" the Pope asked.

"Are you surprised that I'm still alive?" I asked as I tipped my hat to him.

The Pope, who had been smiling, frowned and slowly walked toward us. He got about three feet away from me. "You know you will never get out of here alive," he said.

This was usually the moment when my adrenaline and my fight or flight response would have kicked in, but I was just too drained to care at this point. I took out the two packets of papers, throwing one to each side of me. Immediately the cardinals began to pick up the papers and distribute them.

"What you'll find here, Your Holiness, is to the left is the story that Pope Ignatius hid within a part of himself, one of the two biggest secrets of the church. What you have to your right is the decoding of the lights in Egypt. I trust you've seen the videos of the lights already?" I asked.

The Pope took another step toward me. He was grasping the Staff of the Pinecone so tightly I could see his veins bulging.

"What exactly do you think you're doing? Do you have any idea how many resources we have used to try and get rid of you already? Why won't you just die?" he snarled as the cardinals began to gasp.

"I'm here to expose you as a fraud, Aurelio. We know everything. We know about Pope Ignatius being poisoned, we know that you tried to have us killed because of the capstones. We just weren't sure if you knew what was at the bottom of that," I said.

By this point there were audible gasps in the crowd of cardinals as they had been reading these documents.

"Is this true, Your Holiness? Is any of this true?" asked Cardinal DelVecchio, who had just read about Alberto Rivera.

"So what if it's true? Do you honestly think that it would make a difference? This happened almost 1500 years ago!" he screamed.

"And what about the capstones to the pyramids, did you know about that too?" asked Cardinal Sorrentino.

The Pope started looking around the room and realized he was losing the crowd. They were very angry and wanted some answers.

"Look, everything that's been done has been for the benefit of the Church and most importantly the people that follow us. Could you imagine what would happen if this got out in public? The madness? The riots? Tearing our walls down and scrounging the catacombs for the information in our libraries? Do you know how much more is down there? We would all be finished. I cannot," he said, as he stepped towards me again, "and I will not allow that to happen."

"Save your time on this though, Your Holiness. See, I have already documented everything and put it on the

Internet. It's already hit big in my home country, and it's only a matter of time before people start doing their own research and looking into all of this themselves," I said.

"You're not going anywhere," the Pope said. "Cardinals, detain him until the Swiss Guard arrives."

I looked around the room. This was crunch time. But as I waited for them to encircle me, they instead surrounded him. I had not expected that to happen but was pleased. One by one they came up to me and shook my hand and thanked me for everything.

"You're not going to get away with this!" the Pope screamed at me.

"I think it's time you get out of here," the Camerlengo said to me.

"You and me both," I said as I put my hat back on and flicked the brim.

"You know that there will be a significant number of people who will not believe this. It's really your word against the Vatican's, and the Pope has more of an online following than you do, unfortunately," the Camerlengo said.

"I wouldn't be so sure about that." Once again, I lifted my hat and clicked the brim. The Camerlengo leaned in to look at it and noticed that there was a small hole in the center of it.

"Is that what I think it is?" he asked.

"It's a video camera," I said as I clicked the brim. "Goodbye Camerlengo." I walked out of the Vatican and hopped in a cab to the airport.

I got on the private plane, took my hat off and turned it upside down. I took out the microchip and plugged it directly into my laptop. I uploaded the video to my channel and waited for everything to start. I flipped my phone and made a call. I knew where I had to go to next.

Chapter Thirty-Two

I landed in Houston after a long flight directly from Rome. A guy could get used to private air travel. I rented a car and headed to Clinton, where I would see an old familiar friend of mine.

I arrived there after about forty-five minutes of driving and Blur met me outside. He had seen what was going on everywhere. He gave me a huge hug and started laughing like a maniac.

"Just when I think you can't get more impressive. Ha ha. Look at what you've done to this one world government that they tried to establish. Everything is going to go to pieces. How are you doing? You look good. Want a tall boy?" he asked.

"I feel great, no thanks on the beer, I'd like to just get this started."

"You got it," he said, as we walked to his studio. "Oh wait, you were in the air, you have to see this. My crew cued it up for you when you came in," he said, and turned on the TV.

"In what has been the most controversial move to date, Pope Aurora Toss I has stepped down from the papacy, and as you can see from the white smoke in the distance, in the second fastest Conclave to date, Cardinal Sorrentino has been elevated and is soon to take the name Ignatius II, out of respect for the recently deceased Pope who had perished in what is now being described as suspicious circumstances. Though no autopsy can be performed on a Pope, a viral video from the United States explains how one of the Pope's right-hand men, a former Swiss Guard and enforcer, has been behind the poisoning. These reports are unverified at the moment. From St. Peter's Square, this is Jennifer Polizzi."

I watched the clip, then turned back to Blur. He was chugging a can of Bud Light and high-fiving his crew. I kept thinking that Cardinal Sorrentino would be a good Pope. He would deal with these new revelations head on. Maybe he would be able to have a turning point in the Church where it doesn't just hoard information and wealth and actually dialogues with the communities. Still, many people were going to be angry about these revelations, and I truly didn't give a fuck.

"I read your blog about the Zodiac and all the connections. Are you still looking into that?" Blur asked me.

"So, something interesting happened to me. I work for a radio station like you, and it's owned by Sybelline Entertainment. Sybelline were the mystic records from Virgil's Ecologues. More specifically the Fourth

Ecologue which pre-dates Christ but predicts the birth and rise of a boy who would later become divine. This is the story of the rise and the fall of God's Son/Sun again. Now in the Fifth Ecologue, Virgil gives praise to Caesar Augustus and Julius Caesar. Augustus was the first Emperor after Julius Caesar was betrayed. Julius Caesar, which in English translates to July King, which in Astrology the ruling planet of July/Leo is the Sun. This is another poetic embrace of the rise and eventual slaughter of the Sun/Son. It's important to note that the betrayers of both Jesus and Caesar, which are Judas, Cassius and Brutus, are the three people that are in the lowest level of hell in Dante's *Inferno*. Because of these almost mystical esoteric writings, it makes sense why out of everyone in the world's history, Dante Allegheri chose Virgil to be his tour guide through all the layers of hell. Everybody with a divine mind encoded this information in their paintings, their writings, et cetera. It's actually where Novus Ordo Seclorum from the dollar bill comes from," I said.

"Boy, you're too smart for your own good, you know that?" he asked.

"Live in two minutes. Two minutes, Blur," a cameraman said.

"Are you sure you're ready for this?" Blur asked.

"Videos only do so much. I want to share my story with the world, Blur. Thanks for taking me on," I said.

"For you, anytime you ever want to come on. Hell, I'll let you host sometimes if you want to move down to Houston. We can talk about that afterwards," he said.

"Nah, this isn't for me, but I appreciate the offer," I said.

I took a deep breath.

"And we are live with video superstar Graham Newsdon. Graham, I think everybody has seen your videos so far and we just need to know. How the hell did you get involved in this mess?"

I laughed. "Well you know. I was a drunken medical student just cruising by when I got a call that my brother had died." I began telling the story again.

Chapter Thirty-Three

I got home and went into the living room. There was my family waiting for me.

"Hi baby, I just saw your interview with Blur on TV. I heard he reaches five million people a day. That's way more than regular news channels, right?" Hannah said.

"You got that right," I smiled.

"What are you going to do now?" Jackson asked.

"Yeah, what is there to do now? Want to go out and celebrate, Newsdon?" Rosette asked.

"Not yet, guys, I have to do something," I said.

I sat down at the kitchen table and wrote a letter to Jean.

Dear Jean,

As you've probably already seen by now, I've become semi-famous for my videos and my interview. Since you were the one that started this off, I feel like I should be the first to tell you that I am truly sorry about what you were put through, and I will find it in my heart in one way or another to move past it. We're on Summer Street when you get out of prison, which

I think should be soon with everything that is starting to come out about what happened. Come by.

Graham

I showed this to them. Hannah understood, Jackson was indifferent, and Rosette was mad. She'd get over it. I think she knew that things happened and whether there was a choice in the matter of his decision making, he led us to what we found out. I think we are finally at peace.

"So, what are you going to do now, Graham? You're all over the place. You're like a rock star." Jackson asked.

I thought about it for a minute then smiled. "I'm going to write a book about it," I said.

"Can you even write?" Rosette joked.

"Shut up. No, really, I think I'm going to write a book," I said.

"What happens if an agent or a publishing house doesn't pick it up?" Hannah asked.

"I've got three million views on my videos. I'll self-publish that shit if I have to," I said.

"Alright, well, we're going down to the Fours to celebrate, if you want to come with," Rosette said.

"In a little bit, guys," I said, as they walked out the door.

I sat down and turned Blur Slanders on again and watched my interview with him. I never really liked the way I looked on TV, but it is what it is. I opened my laptop. I just wanted to get something down before I met them at the Fours. I finally felt like I was at peace with everything. I started writing.

Chapter 1:

I can't believe I'm about to do this. They're not going to let what I'm about to do slide, and they're definitely going to figure out how to kill me for it. You think I'm dramatic, don't you? But see, I'm not. Before I get too far ahead of myself, my name is Graham Newsdon and I know the answer to the world's deepest secret.

I paused and closed my computer, got my vest and put it on as I headed out the door to meet them at the bar.

Coming December 15, 2020

Into the Rabbit Hole
The Secret Weapon
By Micah T. Dank

The Secret Weapon, Book Three, the continuation of *Into the Rabbit Hole*: After discovering the True purpose of the Pyramids of Giza as pure energy communication devices, Graham and his group are once again thrown into a hard to believe story. The Rosicrucian's and the Knights Templar long thought to be extinct have been fighting over a secret communication device for the last Thousand years that would allow them to communicate back with the entities that have been sending down messages since the capstones have been restored. Graham and his friends must navigate their way to retrieve this device while being threatened with extinction. The meaning of life is at stake.

For more information
visit: www.SpeakingVolumes.us

Made in United States
Orlando, FL
29 November 2023

39774932R00155